Thief of Hearts

by

Pam Binder

Matchmaker Café Series
Book Four

Thief of Hearts

Cover Art by *Kristian Norris*

The Wild Rose Press, Inc.
PO Box 708
Adams Basin, NY 14410-0708
Visit us at www.thewildrosepress.com

Publishing History
First Fantasy Rose Edition, 2018
Print ISBN 978-1-5092-2247-6
Digital ISBN 978-1-5092-2248-3

Matchmaker Café Series, Book Four
Published in the United States of America

Dedication

To my good friend and critique partner,
Darcy Carson.
Thank you for your wisdom and advice.
You help my stories come alive.

Acknowledgements

Thank you to Rhonda Penders of The Wild Rose Press, for helping make authors' dreams come true.

A special thank you to Nan Swanson, my wonderful editor at Wild Rose Press. Thank you so much for your expert advice on *Thief of Hearts*, and all the books in my Matchmaker Café series. They are better books because of you.

Three days later, Hunter adjusted the backpack on his shoulder as he waited beside the limo that would take Genevieve and him to the airport. He'd happily have ridden the bus into Seattle, but he guessed Genevieve was not the bus kind of gal. Actually, he didn't know what she was really like. She'd ridden a bicycle to their meeting, so it was a high possibility that he hadn't a clue about her.

Which made what he was doing insane. He'd considered backing out and finding another way to investigate whether the matchmaker sisters were running a theft ring, but all the plans he'd come up with weren't as good as this one. He and Genevieve would pretend to be girlfriend and boyfriend on the sisters' Italy tour while they gathered evidence.

Genevieve walked out of the apartment building, pulling a suitcase that looked big enough to carry a body. She wore a figure-hugging sleeveless white dress and four-inch heels. It was a ten-hour flight to London and another five, counting the layover, to Rome. He'd opted for comfort, wearing jeans and a T-shirt. He disagreed with her choice but admitted he enjoyed the view. Genevieve was a fine-looking woman. Down, boy, he cautioned. Remember the last time you fell for a pretty face? Armageddon.

Praise for Pam Binder

"Pam Binder gracefully weaves elements of humor, magic and romantic tension."

Awards
2018 Romantic Times
Pioneers of Romance Fiction Award
for helping forge the way for the many subgenres
in romance.

~

FALLING IN LOVE WITH EMMA was a 2018 finalist
in the Desert Rose RWA, Golden Quill Contest

~*~

Books in the Matchmaker Café Series
MATCH MADE IN THE HIGHLANDS
A BRIDE FOR A DAY
FALLING IN LOVE WITH EMMA
THIEF OF HEARTS
CHRISTMAS KNIGHT
IRISH LOVE SONG

Chapter One

Hunter Longfellow sprinted down a dark alley in Seattle, Washington's Pioneer Square, in a downpour, a neon bar sign and the occasional patrol car his only light. It was a little after ten o'clock in the evening, early for the night-clubbers, but way past bedtime for the kids he'd been asked to locate. This was old Seattle, a tourist haven by day and something else entirely by night. Pioneer Square had its tall brick buildings that had survived Seattle's earthquakes, alleyways that were something out of a Jekyll and Hyde movie, mangy cats, and people who looked out from behind closed doors. The thirteen- and fourteen-year-old kids couldn't have picked a scarier place to hide.

On the street at the end of the alley, another patrol car eased past, slowed, and then continued on its way.

He glanced at the text he'd received from his ex-girlfriend that morning. Mary was a middle school teacher, married now and with a second child on the way. She'd wanted to know if he'd found her students. He texted her that he was closing in, then hoped he was right. He pocketed his cell as the same patrol car swept past again. Coincidence? Or were they following the same lead he had?

Mary and he had remained friends after their break-up, which surprised him, and she invited him to share all the holidays with her family that normal people celebrated. He didn't always attend, but the invitations hadn't stopped.

He reached the address her clues had indicated. It was the last door on his left before the alley dead-ended into a brick wall.

Time to make his move.

He tried the doorknob. Unlocked, which proved his theory that those inside were amateurs. Agitated voices rose behind the door. He calculated he had two options: enter with guns blazing and scare them out of a year's growth, or pretend he was a lost tourist.

He chose option three—the direct approach.

He slammed the door open. It banged against the wall and sent dust and broken cobwebs flying into the air. The room was lit by a single bulb that dangled from the ceiling on a dirty cord. Three boys, ages twelve to fourteen and still dressed in their school uniforms, surrounded the Native American mask they'd stolen from the Burke Museum. They looked in his direction and froze.

He admired their choice. The wood mask represented the creator-eagle of the Makah tribe and was designed to fit over a dancer's head. He'd promised Mary he would find the mask and return it to its rightful owners. He paused, the words "rightful owners" thundering through his thoughts. His father would have said that the hundred-year-old mask belonged with their people, not in a museum.

"Hello, boys," Hunter said.

The teenagers' eyes were wide, and their mouths gaped like fish gasping for breath. One boy fainted and a second shook like a Nordic wind had blown into the room. The third held his ground, a tall, beefy-looking kid with broad shoulders and a world-owes-me expression in his gaze.

Hunter didn't need to ask why the boys had stolen the mask. Mary had filled him in on the story, as well as given him pictures of John, Cory, and T.J. One of them had had the good sense to text Mary for help. The why had involved the school bully, T.J, who Hunter guessed was the one acting like a tough guy. T.J.'s specialty was threatening kids with harming their siblings if they didn't do his bidding.

"Get out of here, Indian," T.J. said.

Hunter stifled a laugh. Classic bully tactics, using name-calling to push the enemy off balance. He ignored T.J. and focused on the one he recognized from the picture as John. "You okay?"

John's expression brightened as he nodded and helped the boy who'd fainted to stand. "I knew you'd come."

T.J. moved to block the view of the mask. "Unless this guy is here to help negotiate a higher price for the mask, I'm not interested."

"We have to give the mask back," John said. "Mrs. Woolhousen said…"

T.J. turned on John, his hand raised. "You called our teacher?"

Hunter closed the distance, stepping between them to block T.J. from John and Cory. Time to cut to the chase. "That's enough, T.J. How soon before your buyers arrive?"

"I'm not telling. They won't like it if the mask isn't here when they get here."

Hunter paused to take another look at T.J. He was the bully on the playground, but who bullied him? That type of behavior usually trickled downhill, like a polluted stream. "We should leave, then." Hunter reached around and grabbed the mask.

"I can't leave," T.J. said, his voice, for once, sounding more like a kid's.

Hunter nodded to the door. "We're all leaving together. I don't leave people behind. And, T.J., you and I will have a chat about your buyers. I'll make sure they don't bother you again."

"Are you going to arrest us?" Cory said, finding his voice.

"I'm not the police. I'm the guy who's here to help you return the mask to the museum."

Chapter Two

The next afternoon, across town, Genevieve Grey, reporter for the *Daily Beat*'s society page, was rushing to her assignment to cover a wedding. She was late. Lately it seemed she was always late. That wasn't like her. She hadn't lost her desire to find the core of a story, but she just wished the stories she covered weren't usually so predictable.

The threat of rain had driven the wedding guests under a canopy of tents lit by thousands of twinkling pink and silver lights while guests waited for the bride's entrance. Genevieve fast-walked past them on three-inch heels to the entrance to the Matchmaker Café. Nestled beneath the Cascade Mountains, in the heart of a retail area nicknamed the Village, the café prepared for a wedding of one of its owners, Fiona McBride, a fitting name on a day like today.

Genevieve slipped into the café and nodded at the bride, who stood in the middle of the room looking more like a statue carved out of white marble than a flesh-and-blood woman. Fiona had sent Genevieve daily updates over the past few months, so all there was left to do was to take notes and await the ceremony. Later, she'd fill in whether or not the bride-to-be was happy or resigned, as right now it was difficult to tell.

Was that how someone would describe her expression when—or if—her fiancé ever got around to picking a wedding date? Was that the reason she'd lost her interest in covering weddings, or was it something else? When she was a student in the journalism department at the University of Washington, her professors called her fearless when she was tracking down a story. When had she lost her edge?

Genevieve washed the prickly thoughts from her mind and concentrated on the bride, continuing to take notes. The bride's dress was borrowed, and yet the fabric fit her body like liquid silk, as though made for her by magical creatures. Fiona was the youngest of the three sisters who owned the café housing their unique matchmaking business. Fiona's blonde hair was pulled away from her face into a bun, giving her a smooth, sophisticated look, but the knuckles of her tightly clenched hands at her sides shone as white as her dress.

Although the bride looked calm now, little things had gone wrong, a situation not unexpected, in Genevieve's experience. The roses were a peach shade instead of the requested blush color. The wedding cake had arrived, but the decorations were not as requested. Ropes of frosting were shaped like ivy and swirled around the five-tiered cake instead of white and silver seashells.

What was not expected by anyone was that the groom couldn't find the bride's ring.

"He's an idiot."

Hearing Lady Roselyn's comment, Genevieve kept her focus on watching the guests arrive from her vantage point near a bay window. Lady Roselyn was the eldest of the three sisters and insisted people address her by her title. Genevieve had learned early in her career that a key to covering a wedding or engagement party was to keep as invisible as possible.

Lady Roselyn had made this same "He's an idiot" comment regarding the groom at least a half-dozen times over the last few minutes, and each time her voice had risen higher. She paced the length of the café, her ankle-length, summer-sky-blue gown swishing around her.

"We could postpone the wedding until the ring is found," said Bridget, the middle sister. She normally wore cream or white but had felt it wasn't appropriate to compete with the bride and had chosen a dress of pale, buttercup-yellow chiffon.

Lady Roselyn stopped pacing, looking like a teakettle ready to explode. "Bite your tongue. Fiona and Liam have postponed this wedding too many times already. Find a ring. We must have something that will work."

Fiona rose from the sofa and moved to stand beside Genevieve. She moved fluidly, as though her feet barely touched the ground. "I apologize. You must think we're horrid. I'm sure the weddings you cover are never this chaotic."

Genevieve smiled, fingering a gold chain around her neck. "You'd be surprised, but I may have a solution for your ring problem." Genevieve removed the chain and slipped off a ring with a sapphire stone in the center. "It belonged to my grandmother. You're welcome to borrow it for the wedding."

Emotion flooded Fiona's expression as tears pooled in her eyes. "You barely know me."

Genevieve squeezed Fiona's hand. "Women should stick together. That's the advice I heard growing up, from both my mother and grandmother. The ring will bring you luck." Genevieve placed the ring in the palm of Fiona's hand. "It will be both something blue and something borrowed."

A carved wooden door toward the back of the café opened. From Genevieve's vantage point, the sky beyond the open door looked as though it were the dead of night instead of two o'clock in the afternoon. Everyone in the café turned toward the sound.

Standing on the threshold was a petite young woman with short-cropped hair and a heart-shaped face. She was barefoot, in a dress of layers of apple-green and butterfly-purple silk.

Bridget shouted with joy and rushed over to the young woman, wrapping her in a warm embrace.

Fiona smiled for the first time. "It is great to see Nissa after all these years. I'm thrilled that she's come for my wedding, but I'm still surprised she's here. She always said she hated big cities."

Lady Roselyn said, "News reached our half-sister that you were getting married. Like the rest of us, Nissa is a matchmaker at heart. She knew you wouldn't go on a honeymoon with Liam unless there was someone to take your place. Our family's rules state that there must be three sisters to help coordinate our tours and our matchmaking."

Fiona closed her hand around the ring and smiled toward Genevieve. "Things are about to get interesting. Come, I'll introduce you to our half-sister. I know you'll like her."

Chapter Three

A few days later, Lady Roselyn walked down to the creek, searching for alone time, and chose the wooden bench near the grassy bank. A rain squall had blown through the area the night before and left the morning smelling fresh and clean.

Fiona and Liam's wedding had been a fantasy come true. She had never seen her sister Fiona happier or more in love. While Fiona and Liam were on their honeymoon, their half-sister Nissa fit in as comfortably as a favorite pair of slippers, and the sisters' matchmaking business had a new romance tour nearly booked and ready for its launch. They had room for one more couple, but Nissa said she already knew who would fill the spot. Lady Roselyn hadn't asked how she knew. Nissa was like Fiona and had a romantic sense about these things.

And to put icing on the cake, Andrew, the man who'd been sent by the Matchmaker Council to review them, had given them his seal of approval and returned to headquarters.

An unusual sound disturbed her quiet thoughts, and she looked up from her journal. Why was it that even after all these years she could always sense Claude's presence?

She turned as he came into view. He was tall, straight, with well-groomed hair, and as dashing as the first time they'd met: the eve of their wedding day. She'd fallen in love with him at first sight. Her euphoria had lasted throughout the wedding ceremony and the month-long honeymoon they'd spent in the south of France. If she could pinpoint a change in how she felt, it would have to be the day they returned. On that day, she'd announced that she and her sisters would continue their hereditary positions as matchmakers. Claude had wanted her to relinquish her position and put him in charge.

"You're not welcome here." Her voice was sharp. She was no longer that young, naïve girl in her twenties.

"Sitting next to you by the creek, or in general?" His voice was silk, his eyes velvet. "I brought you a present. A peace offering."

"It's too late for gifts."

He walked over and placed a square box on her bench and lifted the lid. A heart-shaped cameo brooch surrounded by diamonds lay cushioned in black tissue. The woman's expression, carved from the inside of a mother-of-pearl shell, looked pensive, as though she wondered if she could ever trust again.

Lady Roselyn knew each hand-carved cameo was unique, as though it had a story to tell. In many ways they were like people. She blinked, swiping at the moisture on her cheeks, surprised at the sudden rush of emotion.

"I remembered you liked them," he said.

She let out a hollow laugh. He knew her too well. She closed the lid of the cameo box. "Did you win this in a poker game?"

He chewed on his lower lip as though fighting back

an angry response. "I don't gamble anymore. It's an expensive habit. It makes a person vulnerable."

She nodded slowly, pushing the box aside. "I've filed for divorce."

"I heard, and that's why I'm here. I won't contest. You have every right to ask for a divorce."

"You tried to kill me."

He looked over at the creek. "I could say the same of you. I was young, angry, and full of misguided ambition. I regret what happened between us. I'm a changed man."

She clenched her hands in her lap. Could people really change? She cleared her throat. "What about the doors? The doors in the café are supposed to open into magical adventures back in time, adventures that we control. Instead we no longer know where our couples will end up. Until the issue is resolved, we've resorted to matchmaking tours."

"I know you blame me for the doors malfunctioning, but how could it be me? The doors are enchanted. I wouldn't know how to change anything about them. You have to believe me."

"No, Claude, I don't have to believe you."

Chapter Four

One week later, a spring thunderstorm, followed by a torrential downpour, reminded the Pacific Northwest the reason there were so many trees and flowers—it rained...a lot. The wedding was a distant sweet memory. After the ring mishap, the ceremony had gone off smoothly, and Genevieve's ring had been returned, but she almost wished it hadn't been. She thought her grandmother would have liked the idea of Fiona having the ring.

Genevieve huddled under her apple-green umbrella as she read a newspaper article and waited in line at her favorite bakery in the Village: Emma's Boulangerie. Genevieve had grown up nearby and knew all the owners in the Village, Emma's bakery included. Genevieve wouldn't think of going anywhere else. Those in the Village were like her family.

She was meeting her fiancé, Frank Griffin, and if history were any indicator, he was already inside. He liked being early. Frank also worked at the *Daily Beat* and for some reason wanted to meet with her this morning.

Frank had joined the paper five years ago and had quickly gained the owner's trust. It wasn't that Frank didn't deserve the vote of confidence; it was that Genevieve felt pushed aside, since the owner was her mother. She didn't blame her. Genevieve had never showed interest in assuming more responsibility, mostly because she felt awkward broaching the topic. She didn't want her mother to think that her daughter's interest in running the newspaper meant she wanted her mother to step down. Watching Frank move further into a take-over position over the past year had left her conflicted. Shouldn't she be happy her fiancé and future husband would soon be running the *Daily Beat*?

She shook away what she considered foolish thoughts. She just wished… She paused, remembering an old phrase her grandmother would say: If wishes were wings, we could all fly.

Genevieve edged forward a whole inch and realized the rule was true that when you were late for an appointment there was always a long line to buy a latté and a warm pastry.

But if she didn't get inside soon, her shoes would be ruined, and her black suit soaked down to her skin. Not a great way to start her day. Genevieve tried to position her umbrella better to avoid the rain, but the wind made it difficult. She tried again—and hit the guy in front of her in the shoulders.

Her first impression was that the man was basketball-player tall. She had to look up, which at her height of an even six feet in high heels was not that common. He wore a leather jacket and blue jeans and held a motorcycle helmet at his side. He also had shaggy black hair that looked like he'd cut it himself. Definitely not her type.

He turned storm-gray eyes in her direction.

"Sorry," she said, lifting her umbrella higher. "Would you like to share? There's plenty of room under here for the both of us."

His eyes lightened a shade for an instant before he shook his head. "I like the rain. It's cleansing. Not so great for paper, however. Your newspaper is soaked. There's a new thing called the Internet where people are getting their news," he said with a glint of mischief in his eyes.

She folded the soggy paper and tucked it under her arm. "Hilarious, but for some reason this reporter's articles read better on the printed page. I'm kind of a fan. I've read everything Hunter Longfellow has written. This one involves one of two heart-shaped medallions stolen off Anna Maria de' Medici's body when they exhumed it recently. Anna Maria was the last of the Medici family and died in seventeen hundred forty-three, but the cause of death was never confirmed. Mr. Longfellow is sort of a treasure hunter for hire, but he also works for museums and on archeology sites when paintings and artifacts are stolen. He's a hero, a real-life Indiana Jones."

"Hero?" He rolled his eyes. "How do you know this guy isn't doing it for money and fame?"

Genevieve looked away, offended by the man's reaction to her idol. But it served her right for sharing one of her guilty pleasures with a perfect stranger. Frank said one of her faults was that she shared too much. She pressed her lips together and raised her voice to a level she hoped sounded intimidating. "You wouldn't understand. Hunter Longfellow is not a mercenary, and I admire him very much. He makes sure that the world's great art is protected from those who would steal it for their own pleasure. Besides, Mr. Longfellow doesn't like to be photographed, so no one really knows what he looks like. Does that sound like a man who is in it for the money and fame?"

The man simply raised an eyebrow as the line edged forward, plunging the morning into silence once again.

"I wouldn't mind sharing your umbrella," an elderly gentleman said.

"Mr. Digby," Genevieve said, positioning her umbrella to include him. "Of course. I'm sorry I didn't see you sooner." It was common gossip in the Village that Mr. Digby, who dressed in wool slacks and a sports jacket in the style of the nineteen fifties, was dating Gigi, the bakery owner's grandmother.

"Aren't you usually at the bakery earlier?"

"Gigi wouldn't have it. With Emma away on a buying spree in Europe, they're short staffed, and Gigi said I'd be a distraction." He grinned. "Imagine a man my age being a distraction to such a fine lady like Gigi."

When he mentioned Gigi, his face glowed. Genevieve couldn't help herself. She reached down and gave him a big hug.

A man behind her and Mr. Digby asked him a question about the French Revolution, one of his passions, and the conversation turned to weapons and warfare strategies.

The line inched closer to the bakery's entrance. She could leave and go to one of the zillion other coffee shops in the area, but she'd convinced her fiancé to meet her here, and he didn't like it when she changed her plans. Besides, she needed the winning combination of sugar and caffeine to start her day. Translation: For maintaining a reporter's objective tone and facial expression while conducting an interview with even the most outrageous celebrity, caffeine and sugar were paramount. If there were chocolate involved...even better.

Although, in this circumstance, she didn't need that much fortification, as she was looking forward to the interview with the matchmaker sisters. After her original feature on them, plus the report on the wedding, the sisters had become celebrities, and people wanted to learn more.

The line slogged forward until she was inside the cozy warmth of the bakery and surrounded by the smells of baked bread, cinnamon, and chocolate, as well as the rumble of conversation. Mr. Digby nodded his thanks to Genevieve for sharing her umbrella and headed toward the counter to greet Gigi.

Still in line, Genevieve folded her umbrella. People didn't seem to mind the long wait, and Genevieve attributed it to the welcoming atmosphere the owners created. There was a sense of timelessness to the room. The bakery had a French feel with its round tables, crisp linens, and vintage wallpaper that depicted scenes of eighteenth- and nineteenth-century Paris.

Caitlin and Catherine, eight-year-old twins with bouncing curls and dressed in a froth of pink and purple, passed out trays of samples as the line crawled toward the counter. Their mother, Dora, who was an older version of her daughters, was behind the counter helping Gigi. Both women wore crisp white aprons over their dresses and met each customer with a smile. Gigi always reminded Genevieve of how Mrs. Santa Claus might look. Gigi's cheeks were a soft rose-pink, and she always had a kind word for everyone she met.

When Caitlin approached, Genevieve leaned over,

selected a sample of a blueberry muffin, and nodded a thank you.

The child's face beamed like sunshine. "Gigi said my sister and I are a big help."

"I don't doubt it for a minute."

And then, surprise, surprise, Genevieve was next in line, just one more person ahead of her.

The next instant, the man at the counter, the same one she'd bonked with her umbrella, spoke in a deep voice, drawing her attention. His voice reminded Genevieve of thunder rumbling over a quiet evening. "Two scones and two lattés," he said, tucking his helmet under his arm as he reached for his wallet.

The bakery's dog, Mocha, a golden retriever with happy brown eyes, bounded toward the man as he accepted his order from Gigi. In the next instant, Mocha stood on hind legs and put front paws on the man's chest, trying to reach the plate of scones. The man spun around, trying to keep his lattés and food out of Mocha's reach, but as he backed up his shoulder glanced against Genevieve's.

Everything seemed to happen in slow motion.

As the drinks sloshed over their cup rims, the scones slid off the plate onto the floor—to Mocha's delight. The dog gave a yelp of joy and pounced on the fallen treats.

Genevieve spun around on her heels to get out of the way, dropping her purse and umbrella. Tipped off balance, she flailed her arms like a manic windmill and began to fall.

The man caught her before she touched the ground, holding her in his arms as time slowed. She noticed his lashes were ridiculously long. Why was it that men's eyelashes were thick, while most women had to apply layers of mascara or endure applying false eyelashes to achieve the same look? It wasn't fair. And then she saw the intense fear reflected in his storm-gray eyes, as though he'd hurt her somehow.

"It's not your fault," she felt compelled to say. "You saved me."

He righted her as though she were nothing more substantial than a stuffed animal and mumbled something that sounded like an apology. He stood with his hands on her waist, then nodded and headed away toward a table at the far corner of the bakery. The woman he greeted was wearing an adorable black raincoat with rust piping, but Genevieve couldn't see the woman's face.

Genevieve stared after him. "That was odd."

Gigi came from around the counter, holding a cloth that she handed to Genevieve. "Oh, my, he spilled coffee all over your lovely suit. Are you all right, dear?"

"I'm…yes…I mean…" Genevieve turned toward Gigi, trying to dislodge the experience, but the look in the man's gaze lingered in her mind. Vulnerable. Kind.

Gigi handed Genevieve a latté. "Your fiancé has a table for you in the back of the bakery."

"Who?" She took a deep breath. "Oh, Frank. Right. Thank you." She headed in the direction Gigi indicated, set her latté on the table, and placed her shoulder bag over the chair rail.

As she sat down, Frank looked up from reading the messages on his phone. He took a few seconds to look her over. "You're a mess, and the bakery's dog followed you over. Tell it to leave. We have to talk."

Chapter Five

The whirring sound of coffee brewing blended with conversation as Hunter joined his friend Mary at the corner table. Gigi had replaced the lattés and scones, with her apology and the promise to scold Mocha. She didn't know what had gotten into the dog. According to Gigi, he'd never acted that way before.

Hunter accepted both the apology and the scones with a nod, looking for the woman he'd held in his arms. He was cutting it close for his next assignment, but he'd promised to meet Mary and give her an update.

He scanned the bakery, infused as it was with the aromas of coffee, chocolate, and fresh-baked scones and muffins, crowded with people conducting interviews, working on their computers, meeting friends, writing their novels, and parents playing with their children in a "kid friendly" section. He'd expected the bakery to have a teeth-clenching noise, like fingernails on a blackboard. Instead it was restful. Then he saw her. The woman he'd bumped into. Twice. She was sitting toward the back of the bakery, her long, raven-black hair tied back into a ponytail, talking to a guy in a suit the color of shark skin. Her expression reminded him of the Mona Lisa, and for some reason he had the overwhelming impulse to try and make her smile.

"Earth to Hunter," his friend Mary said.

He reached for a scone. "Sorry."

He and Mary had broken up six years ago—or was it seven or eight? He'd lost track of time. She looked the same as he remembered when he'd been invited over for Thanksgiving a few years ago. Her dark hair was medium length, she had a never-ending smile, and she was pregnant with her second child. Her husband was one of the good guys and made her happy. He'd even let Hunter rant that the first Thanksgiving between the Wampanoag tribe and the Pilgrims of Plymouth Colony in sixteen hundred and twenty-one wasn't as big a deal back then as we made it out today.

Hunter took a long pull on his latté. "Where's Sir Rug-Rat?"

She chuckled and pinched off a corner of her scone. "He is with the other three-year-olds at the children's music academy next door. You know very well his name is Bradley. You must stop calling him Sir Rug-Rat. He thinks it's a cooler name than Bradley."

"Smart kid."

She rolled her eyes. "Anyway, this morning at breakfast Bradley announced he wanted to start a band."

Just then Mocha trotted over and flopped down next to Hunter as though they were old friends. Hunter reached down and scratched the dog behind the ear. "How does your lawyer husband feel about that?"

"He asked our son if he could be the drummer."

Hunter took a drink of his latté. "Your husband's a good man."

Mary nodded over toward the dog that leaned against Hunter's leg and had fallen asleep.

"So are you. Animals and kids love you. You have

a big heart, and they sense it."

He chuckled under his breath. "Animals and kids? That sounds about right."

"You know what I mean. I wish you'd give people a chance. They might surprise you. The woman you bumped into a few minutes ago, for instance. Her name's Genevieve. We went to college together. I could introduce you to her."

"Not interested."

"Could have fooled me." She sipped her latté. "Thank you for helping my students."

Mocha lifted on his haunches and rested his head on Hunter's knee, pushing his head against Hunter's hand. Hunter obliged, rubbing the dog under his chin. "I didn't do anything special. I was there at the right time, is all."

"Minimize it if you like, but because of you, the mask was returned, the charges dropped in exchange for community service working at the Burke Museum, and the high school thugs harassing T.J. were arrested. Now, if you could have that same success with your love life…" She let the sentence drift. "I worry about you."

"I'm fine."

She paused again, her gaze lingering on him. "I almost forgot. The boys picked out a thank-you present for you. It was T.J.'s idea."

"I hate gifts."

"Too late." Mary reached into her tote-size purse and pulled out a small box with the Burke Museum logo. "I promised them you'd wear it." She pulled out a forest-green stone pendant suspended on a rope of black leather and slipped it around Hunter's neck, despite his grumbling protest.

He flipped the stone over and traced his thumb over the engraved word.

"The boys said the person who sold them the pendent at the museum didn't know what the word meant." She smiled. "Maybe it means fine?"

"Good one." He tucked the pendant under his black T-shirt. "Change of topic. What do you know about the Matchmaker Café in the Village?"

Mary coughed, covering her mouth with her hand. "Why didn't you tell me you're looking for a matchmaker?"

Hunter glanced over his shoulder, thankful for the steady hum of conversation in the bakery. "Lower your voice. I'm on assignment, and I need a little background information about the matchmakers and their tours."

Mary sat back in her chair and heaved a sigh. "Well, if you ever do, you know, feel in the mood for a set-up, I have a gaggle of single girlfriends and teacher friends."

"You'll be my first contact. Information, please."

She sat forward. "Okay, the three sisters, Lady Roselyn, Bridget, and Fiona. run the Matchmaker Café, and everyone in the Village loves them. Besides being friendly, they've brought in a lot of business. The sisters offer a variety of adventures and tours, depending on the wishes of the individual or couple. People who've been on one of these tours, or adventures, say they felt as though they'd visited another time and place. The sisters promise they can find a person's soulmate, deepen relationships, or turn a friendship into happily-ever-after. It's all very romantic, and some whisper there's a touch of magic, which brings me to my question. You track down thieves of antiquities, not couples looking for connections. What exactly is your assignment? Is it dangerous?"

Hunter glanced at the time on his phone. "Can't say, but what you just told me is useful." He leaned over and gave her a peck on the cheek. "Take care of the Rug-Rat and the new one on the way. I should be gone only a week, but I'll check in with you when I return."

"Good, that will give me more than enough time to find you someone nice to date."

Chapter Six

When a man says, "We have to talk," it usually means a break-up. What Genevieve had discovered in her relationship with Frank was that it meant something else entirely. It meant a lecture, and today was no exception.

She had endured it for the last half hour, listening to Frank lecture to her about how he intended to change the newspaper that had been in her family for almost a century. She knew Frank meant well, because he said that exact phrase at the beginning of these "talks." Normally, it didn't bother her, but today it did. She should have requested an extra shot of chocolate in her latté.

She settled back in her chair and drank the last of her coffee. "I'm assuming you'll want a report on the matchmaker article when I'm finished. I'm meeting with the sisters this morning."

He either hadn't heard the deep sarcasm in her tone or chose to ignore it. "Your mother is still living in the past," he said. "People don't read gossip in newspapers anymore. They read it online. If they do buy a newspaper, they want blood, violence, corruption, and scandal. You write puff pieces."

Genevieve buttoned the top button of her suit jacket. "It's what my mother wants, and she relies on me to deliver. You might be the manager of the *Daily*

Beat, but my mom is the owner. She's been running the newspaper since she took it over from her father, who took it over from his father before him, and she likes my column."

"She likes you." Frank let out his breath. "Things change. If you want to survive, you change with the times."

Genevieve leaned forward as a shiver of panic ran through her. It was the same fear she knew newspapers across the country faced these days. "Is someone trying to buy the newspaper? Is that why you wanted to meet this morning?"

"That dog is back." He pulled his gaze from the dog to her. "I think we should delay setting a wedding date until we know for sure."

Genevieve rubbed the ring finger on her left hand. He'd never given her an engagement ring, saying that he wanted to surprise her with a large diamond solitaire when they exchanged vows. "You want to delay setting a date…again? Frank, if you don't want to marry me, just say so."

Frank reached for her hands. "Of course I want to marry you. I love you. Don't be like that, Ginny. There is so much going on right now, and I want to make sure I'll be able to help you with the wedding preparations. I don't want you to turn into one of those bridezillas you write about in your columns."

She hated it when he called her Ginny. She'd told him once that Genevieve was her grandmother's name and every time she heard it she was reminded of the kind and generous lady with the big heart. His response was that all couples had nicknames for each other. So far, she hadn't picked a nickname for Frank.

She slipped her hands from his. "I appreciate your offer of help at our wedding, but it's not necessary. Plus, I'm hardly the bridezilla type."

"I'm sure all brides say that before they're engaged, and I'm sure you would do a fine job. I only want to help make it perfect for us."

She clasped her hands in her lap. He was offering to help. She should be thankful. Most men wanted nothing to do with choosing flowers or taste-testing the cake. "Do you have a date in mind?"

"That's better. Why don't we discuss it toward the end of the month, when things settle down?" Frank stood. "I'm glad you understand. You need to make your interview, and I have an appointment in Seattle. See you tonight. I might be a little late. I'm not sure how long my meeting will last."

She nodded and watched as he maneuvered around Mocha, who had stubbornly refused to move out of Frank's way.

Genevieve waited until Frank had disappeared out the door, then reached down and scratched Mocha behind the ear. "What do you think that was all about? You don't have to answer. This is the third time Frank has delayed our wedding date. I'm a reporter, even if the only articles I write are about engagements and weddings. How cliché that the expert on dating and men is in denial that there is a real possibility that her fiancé is cheating on her."

Mocha licked Genevieve's hand, and she smiled and gave him a hug around his neck. "Yes, I love you too. Let's see if Gigi has any chocolate croissants left."

As Genevieve reached the counter, she overheard Gigi mention they were shorthanded. Daisy, one of the staff, had taken a day off to prepare for a trip, and they hadn't been able to find a replacement.

Genevieve decided a little good will would keep her distracted from thoughts of the possibility that Frank would never set a wedding date and their family newspaper faced buy-out or worse. Not to mention thoughts of the hunky guy who'd saved her from falling. What was it about that guy? Yes, he was good-looking. No contest on that score. But there was more. There was a depth in his eyes that made her want to learn more about him.

She mentally shook free of him. He was a stranger. She'd never see him again.

"I'd be glad to help," she blurted before she could change her mind.

"Me too," Mary chimed in from behind Genevieve.

"Mary!" Genevieve squealed, pulling her college friend into her embrace. "I thought you were living back east. Why didn't you tell me you'd returned?"

Mary hugged Genevieve. "The last time we were together, you said you never wanted to see me again."

Genevieve shook her head and laughed. "Did I really say something that silly? That sounds like me. In my defense, Chad had just asked you to his fraternity's spring fling, not me. I was crushed. What was his last name again?"

Mary laughed. "I can't remember either."

Gigi handed both Mary and Genevieve aprons and indicated they should follow her into the kitchen to help fill orders.

While she walked, Genevieve tied on the bib-style apron. "So, catch me up."

Mary patted her tummy. "Obviously pregnant. This

will be baby number two. My husband is from the East Coast but wanted to set up his law practice in Seattle, and I met him shortly after I accepted a job to teach at one of the middle schools here."

"Wait, I think I remember seeing you when I came in, or the back of you, anyway. I remember liking your raincoat. A man brought you latté and scones. Was that your husband?"

Mary scrunched her eyebrows together. "Oh, you must mean Hunter Longfellow. No, we're just good friends."

Genevieve felt as though the floor had dropped out from under her. She'd gushed over the Hunter Longfellow article, never realizing that she was gushing to the author. She groaned, knowing she'd made a fool of herself. Maybe they weren't the same man... "Curious, but is that the same Hunter Longfellow who travels the globe like the main character in the Indiana Jones movies, although his alter ego is a Pulitzer Prize-winning writer, not a professor?"

"That's Hunter."

Gigi handed Genevieve a tray of pastries with instructions to deliver them to table three, then a similar tray to Mary for table five.

As Genevieve and Mary headed off to deliver the orders, Mary turned toward Genevieve with a wink. "Hunter's single."

Chapter Seven

Hunter slipped into the Matchmaker Café behind a man he recognized. Jorvy Erickson and his brother Björn were co-owners of the Pisces Fish Market. Jorvy hadn't recognized him and seemed focused on talking with Bridget McBride, the middle sister. Hunter knew the youngest, Fiona, was still on her honeymoon.

When Hunter first received a tip on the matchmaker sisters and their tours, he did what he always had—he vetted the story. This meant doing research on anyone in the subject's circle. He knew what the matchmaker sisters looked like, from the feature in the *Daily Beat*. He knew they'd moved here from Scotland, where matchmaking had been the family business for generations. As soon as they'd arrived in Seattle, they'd rented this building, renovated it, and settled into the family of Village retailers as though they'd been here from its nineteen-sixties beginning.

"Can I help you? I'm Lady Roselyn."

He gave a polite nod, but he knew who she was— the eldest sister of the three matchmakers. Dressed in an ankle-length dark blue straight skirt and matching blouse, her only decoration was a diamond brooch pinned below her collar. He surmised the severity of her clothing was by design. According to his research, she insisted that everyone address her as Lady Roselyn. What he didn't know was whether she'd been married to a lord, was descended from a line of nobility, had purchased the title, or simply liked the idea. There was a fire in her eyes that suggested she didn't suffer fools.

He held out his hand. "My name's Hunter Longfellow. "I'm interested in signing up for one of your tours."

"Are you, now? Come along away from the front door. Let's go someplace where we can have a chat. Are you aware that we are not like most matchmaking companies? We like to find out a little about our potential clients before we agree to help them. For example, when a person says they're looking for love, what are they really saying?"

"That they're lonely?" Hunter offered.

Lady Roselyn sat down at one of three empty tables clustered in a corner of the café. Along the wall behind them was a forest-green door that looked like it had once belonged in a country estate in France. On either side was an assortment of photos, shadow boxes that displayed keepsakes, such as watches or jewelry, as well as a child-size tea set. The standout was a framed embroidered image of Scheherazade, clad in gold jewelry and rich fabrics. She was the famed storyteller in the tale of one thousand and one Arabian nights.

"And are you lonely, Mr. Longfellow?" Lady Roselyn motioned for Bridget to bring coffee.

He tore his gaze from the embroidered portrait and settled across from Lady Roselyn. He'd seen it before, but where? He studied the rose-print tablecloth, calculating how to proceed. He'd expected the third degree from Lady Roselyn. He hadn't expected how he'd feel. "Does anyone ever lie to you?"

"All the time."

He grinned. He liked how direct she was. Most people sugar-coated their answers. He tried to formulate an answer that would be in line with what he hoped she wanted, but in his head it all sounded cliché and false. "You have an unusual collection of art."

"Are you an art dealer, Mr. Longfellow?"

He grinned again, accepting the coffee that Bridget had brought them. "Thank you," he said, and to Lady Roselyn he replied, "In a way."

"Do you need my help?" Bridget said to her sister.

"It is all under control," Lady Roselyn said. "Thank you for the coffee and tea."

Hunter took a drink of his coffee. It was bitter and strong, reminding him of Turkish-style coffee, and then he remembered why the portrait of Scheherazade was familiar. He'd seen one exactly like this in his friend's home in Persia. When he commented on it, his friend told him the story of the sultan who had fallen in love with Scheherazade. His friend had the original but never mentioned there were others. Hunter would have to examine this one to be sure, but at just a casual glance, it didn't look like a reproduction.

When Bridget left, Lady Roselyn turned once more to Hunter. "Where were we? Ah, yes, you were about to tell me about your interest in art."

For some reason he had the impression that Lady Roselyn already knew the answer. It was like playing chess. He'd make a move and wait for his opponent's turn. Until he'd seen the framed embroidery of Scheherazade, he'd been on the fence about accepting the assignment to investigate the sisters and their business. Now he was intrigued.

He set his coffee aside. "I'm not an expert on art. I

don't think anyone could claim such a thing. The field is too vast. The most a person could wish for would be to have areas where they could at least hold their own. Even then, there's always something to learn. Take, for example, that framed tapestry of Scheherazade, there behind you. It's stunning. When was it purchased, or are you the person who stitched the image?"

Lady Roselyn turned toward the wall, her eyes laser focused on the image he'd mentioned. "I'd forgotten it was there," she said, so low the words sounded more like a hushed breeze. "It's been in our family for as long as I can remember. I have no idea who the artist was or who purchased it. You are right—everything about it is stunning."

"Scheherazade."

"I beg your pardon?"

Hunter turned the coffee mug slowly in his hand. "Scheherazade. She's both the woman in the portrait and the one who stitched the image, or at least that's the legend. The tree in the background is unusual. It looks like a common apple tree, but in addition to apples, there are pears, oranges, lemons, limes, and several fruits that are now extinct. The original was created thousands of years ago by the greatest storyteller of all time, Scheherazade."

"If memory serves," Lady Roselyn said, "Scheherazade's story was chronicled in *The Arabian Nights*. She was offered as a one-night's entertainment for the sultan, knowing that in the morning she'd be killed. But she was not an ordinary woman. She was smart. She told the sultan a story and ended it on what writers call a hook. He wanted to know the ending. She told him she would tell him the ending the following night. He was caught up in the story and agreed and spared her life. This went on for one thousand and one nights. In the meantime, they had a chance to know each other and fell in love. There have been many studies of the story, but I always wondered at both the sultan's original motives for killing anyone who got too close to him and Scheherazade's insight that stories were more than just the key to her survival."

"The past is not easy to decipher," Hunter said. "She holds on to her secrets. I think that's what drew me to the study of art in the first place. You can learn a lot about people by studying the past."

Lady Roselyn smiled for the first time. "You are not what I expected." She withdrew a card from the cuff of her sleeve and pushed it across the table. "Give this to Bridget. She will know what to do."

Hunter waited until Lady Roselyn left and then glanced at the card. Printed on the card was the Matchmaker Café's logo of a Scottish thistle etched on the image of a door.

Chapter Eight

It had taken longer than Genevieve expected to help Gigi with the customers at the bakery. Genevieve had called the Matchmaker Café and told them she'd be late but could almost hear Frank's voice in her head saying that a reporter worth a grain of salt put his or her work first. Her mother, however, would have approved of her helping Gigi.

Genevieve ran to the Matchmaker Café through the steady downpour. She could imagine the storm clouds laughing as they dumped rain on the silly humans who lacked the common sense to stay inside. Gigi had kept her and Mary busy, which was a good thing. It gave Genevieve a reprieve from thinking too much about Frank, the stranger who'd bumped into her at the bakery, and whether or not she was wasting her time as a reporter for the society page. As usual, she was overthinking her life and her goals. She had a good job and a fiancé. Why did she need to worry?

She shoved open the door to the Matchmaker Café and was greeted with a rush of warm air laced with the gentle fragrance of lavender. It felt bigger inside than the dimensions of the outside of the building suggested. Antique wood tables and chairs in varying sizes and shapes filled the center space where customers poured over brochures. Lines formed in front of a registration desk to Genevieve's right and a buffet table heaving with sweet rolls and fruit on her left.

Lady Roselyn greeted her. "It's wonderful to see you again."

Genevieve held out her hand in greeting but was pulled into a hug.

Lady Roselyn's smile warmed. "My sisters and I are so grateful your newspaper is doing another article." She swept her arm to indicate the room. "As you can see, the ad we placed with your mother resulted in overwhelming success. So much so, we had to add an additional tour to Italy. I didn't have a chance to tell you at Fiona and Liam's wedding, but I love the feature you write, 'The Daily Tattle-Tale.' It's so much fun and the best way to start a person's day. I love your current series on unique celebrity wedding locations. Did an Arabian prince really build a heart-shaped island for his bride-to-be?"

"All true." Genevieve took out her notepad. She was relieved there hadn't been a follow-up article on that story. The bride had rejected the prince when she learned he'd built an identical island close by for his mistress.

"You don't understand," a man at the registration desk was saying, "I have to go on this tour."

Genevieve recognized the deep voice. She looked in the direction of the commotion, and sure enough, it was Hunter Longfellow.

Bridget stood up from the table, her hands placed palms down on its surface as she leaned forward. "And you don't understand. This is a couples-only tour."

"That's ridiculous," Hunter said. "Your tour is advertised as a matchmaking tour. That translates into you finding me a match. I don't bring my own."

Bridget tucked her pen into the loose knot of hair perched on top of her head. "Usually, that would be the case. We're trying something new. We've learned that just because two people are together it doesn't always equate to a happily-ever-after. Life intrudes, and careers get in the way of relationships. This new tour we've created gives couples a second chance to realize why they fell in love in the first place. Again, this is a couples-only tour. No exceptions." She handed Hunter a brochure. "All of the information I've told you is below the packing instructions and conditions."

Lady Roselyn leaned toward Genevieve. "If you'll excuse me, Bridget needs my help." In a matter of seconds, Lady Roselyn appeared beside Hunter, resting a restraining hand on his arm. "I'm very sorry, but we have some romantic adventures that might suit you better. The south of France is lovely this time of year, or the Highlands of Scotland."

"I'll figure something out." He reached for his cell phone and exited the café.

****

That afternoon, Genevieve sat at her desk in the newsroom of the *Daily Beat*, allowing the clatter of phones ringing and voices raised in animated conversation to wash over her. She'd obtained more background information from the sisters regarding their business and why they loved matchmaking. It was all lollipops and rainbows. Any sweeter and she'd have gained weight. Her mother would love the follow-up story. Frank would hate it, and more and more her mother had become dependent on Frank's opinion.

But the sisters hadn't been able to help Hunter Longfellow. And why a man as talented and accomplished as he was didn't have a girlfriend was…was none of her business.

Genevieve glanced at the time and jumped to her feet. Terrific. She was running late. She had to hand the matchmaker story over for approval if she wanted to make deadline. She slipped on the high-heeled pumps she'd discarded under her desk. They pinched her toes, but Frank insisted they made her look more professional. She grabbed the folder and raced through the newsroom.

Well, raced wasn't exactly the right word, considering what she was wearing. Genevieve's pencil skirt was so tight and her heels so high that, if she walked fast at full tilt, she would look like a waddling penguin on stilts. But Frank's motto was that looking the part was more important than comfort.

She made it through the gauntlet of her coworkers without incident. In times past, they would have greeted her, shared news. Now, everyone had their faces pressed close to their monitors as their fingers flew over their keyboards. These days, there was less laughter and more pressure to outperform the online media world.

She paused in front of her mother's office and knocked. In the following brief moment of silence, her mind went back to when, as an eight-year-old, she had announced at Thanksgiving dinner—which had included the two of them, their three cats, and a Scottish Terrier named Scoop—that she wanted to work at the family newspaper. Her mother had been thrilled. She'd asked only that Genevieve adhere to their family's golden rule: find a story's heart.

Genevieve heard her mother's voice from inside the office and entered. "I finished the story you requested…" Genevieve paused. She was talking to an empty room. Odd. She could have sworn she'd heard her mother's voice. Then Genevieve heard giggling.

"David. Stop. Our daughter's here."

Genevieve's mother and stepdad emerged from an alcove, flushed and out of breath, like teenagers caught kissing under the bleachers at a football game. Her mother adjusted the floral scarf she wore at the top of her pink suit, and her stepdad buttoned his tweed sportscoat. They were both about the same height, her mother with her round sunshine face and David, who looked like he was always on the verge of laughter. They were so comfortable around each other that people thought they'd been married and in love for thirty-five years instead of just nine.

Ten years ago, David had responded to a job opening at the newspaper, and a short time later he'd proposed to Genevieve's mother. Genevieve's father had died fighting in Afghanistan when she was six years old, but memories of her father were still vivid. David had said he never wanted to replace her father and had vowed to always be kind and loving and watch over her and her mother. He'd exceeded everyone's expectations. Most of all, he'd made Genevieve's mother smile again.

Her mother smoothed down her shoulder-length red hair. "We weren't expecting you. We thought you'd still be interviewing the sisters at the café. What time is it? One o'clock?"

Genevieve fought back the urge to smile. Her mother had lost track of time. Another positive influence David had on her. "It's almost five. I can come back later."

"No need," David said, walking over to kiss Genevieve on the forehead. "I have a meeting with the University of Washington's new football coach." David blew Genevieve's mother a kiss. "Save the world, honey."

Her mother's cheeks flushed as she blew a kiss to him in return. As David left the office, Frank entered.

He walked in as though he'd already taken over the office. "Dorothy, do you have a minute. I have a few thoughts on the front page."

Dorothy headed toward her desk, still fussing with her hair. "No need. Genevieve finished the follow-up piece on the matchmaker sisters. The feature we did in the Sunday paper under local new businesses was one of our most popular in years."

"If you're talking about the wedding section, I agree. But it's not for the front page. That's for the society page."

"Not everything has to involve disasters," Dorothy said, sitting down behind her desk. "People also want the feel-good story that will start their day with a smile. Genevieve was just about to fill me in on the details. Join us."

"This is not the time to make mistakes," Frank said. "We're taking the *Daily Beat* in a new direction."

"My mother and our family have been running this newspaper for almost a century," Genevieve said. "My mother knows what sort of story fits on the front page. Besides, I saw Hunter Longfellow at the matchmaker café earlier today. He was trying to sign up for one of their tours. That proves my mother's theory that even someone like him wants a little romance in their life."

"Hunter Longfellow? The guy who tracked down

the mercenaries who stole priceless antiquities from a museum in Cairo? That Hunter Longfellow? There is no way he was interested in just a matchmaking tour. He's investigating a story." Frank paused. "What is the angle?"

"He didn't have an angle. In fact, he won't be going on a tour. The tour he wanted was for couples only. He was insistent that it had to be the one leaving for Rome in a few days. He looked pretty steamed when they told him he couldn't go unless he had a significant other."

"Maybe we're not talking about the same guy," Frank said. "How can you be sure it was him? Few have seen him photographed."

"I bumped into a college friend of mine at Emma's bakery after you left. Mary was having coffee with him, and one thing led to another, and she told me that she and Hunter were friends."

"Perfect. Call your friend and ask her for Hunter's contact information. Meet with him. Tell him you'll pose as his girlfriend or wife, or whatever is needed to get you on that tour with him. He's investigating a story, and this is exactly what we need to bring this newspaper back from the brink of extinction."

"Why does Genevieve have to go with this person?" Dorothy said. "You and Genevieve should go. Rome is very romantic. It would be good for the two of you to get away together."

"I can't leave right now," Frank said. "There's too much at stake."

"We don't know if there is a story," Dorothy said. "Poor boy might be lonely."

Frank's mouth lifted in a sneer. "Lonely? He's

single, travels the globe first class compliments of whoever hires him, and speaks a half dozen or more languages. Hunter's not lonely. He's living the dream. Genevieve, I want you to convince Hunter to bring you along."

"If he's all you claim, he's probably already found someone."

Frank turned Genevieve toward the door and gave her a slight shove over the office threshold. "Then your assignment is to convince this Pulitzer Prize-winning writer that you're the better choice."

Chapter Nine

Hunter sped his Harley along West Lake Sammamish Road with the drone of the engine like a meditation mantra in his ears. After his failed attempt to register for the matchmaker's Italy tour, he'd called Mary. At breakfast she'd offered to set him up with one of her single friends. Since the tour was couples only and all the women he knew were married, he felt Mary's suggestion was his best option.

A thick forest of cedar trees, ferns, and rhododendrons lined the road on his left side, and the mirror-smooth lake was to his right. It was dusk, that twilight time the Makah believed was a time between worlds where humans could shift into their animal forms and where anything was possible. Like most legends, Hunter believed there was a little truth around the edges.

He had been thinking about those types of legends a lot lately. Every time he began researching a job, he made it a point to learn as much as possible about the history surrounding the stolen artwork. He didn't claim to be an expert, but he could hold his own. He leaned his bike, taking a curve to the right, noted that the traffic had thinned, and continued mulling his assignment. He'd been given a tip that the matchmaker tours might be a front for a massive art theft ring. His informant's theory was that the tour group would enter a museum or historical site, cause a disturbance, and when the dust settled, and the tour group was long gone, so would be a piece of art.

The concept was intriguing. Despite all the security measures, thieves were always finding ingenious methods to break the system. Even so, Hunter had been skeptical—until he saw the inside of the Matchmaker Café for himself. Lady Roselyn had said the portrait of Scheherazade was a family heirloom. Except he'd seen one like it in the home of his Persian friend. Hunter couldn't be one hundred percent sure, but the embroidery didn't look like a reproduction. It looked like the real deal. Hunter had reached out to his friend in case Scheherazade had created more than one, but so far he hadn't heard back.

A car horn broke his concentration. He motioned for them to go around him and nodded his apology for going below the speed limit.

He glanced in his bike's mirror. Several cars opted to pass him, but one was apparently happy right where it was. It was a nondescript silver sedan like most of the cars on the road, with an ordinary license plate, and a driver who drove the thirty-five-an-hour speed limit like it was a religion. What piqued Hunter's interest was that the driver was wearing sunglasses on a cloudy afternoon. Was the driver following him? Hunter's mild interest in the driver shot to DEFCON three, ready to shift into defensive mode at a moment's notice.

He was close to Mary's house by now, and the last thing he wanted to do was involve Mary and her family in anything that could be dangerous.

The road stretched out before him, and for the moment there wasn't any traffic in either direction. If he was to make a move, it had to be now. He leaned over the handlebars and increased his speed.

The sedan kept pace.

It could be a coincidence, except Hunter had always stayed ahead of the bad guys with the motto that there wasn't such a thing.

Hunter increased his speed again, this time pulling ahead and blowing past the speed limit. The sedan did the same. So, not a coincidence. Time to change direction. Hunter had played this cat-and-mouse game before, as recently as his last trip to Scotland. There a thief had attempted to steal a four-hundred-year-old tin mirror off the wall in Holyroodhouse. The mirror had once belonged to Mary, Queen of Scots, and was nearly priceless. Hunter had been in Edinburgh on another assignment but had been at the right place at the right time. The thief took off on his motorcycle, and so did Hunter, racing up Edinburgh's Royal Mile. No one had been hurt, and the press explained it as tourists gone wild, but Hunter never liked it when his suspect was loose amongst innocents.

Time to lose this guy.

Hunter simultaneously leaned his body to the left and pressed down on the left handlebar grip, steering his bike into a U-turn. The engine roared and the tires squealed as he made the maneuver and sped past the sedan on the opposite side of the road.

Out of the corner of his eye, Hunter saw the man glance in his direction as they passed each other, and he caught a good look at the man: Caucasian, focused expression, sharp-edged cheekbones, and a military-style haircut. Hunter turned up a steep road on his right that angled away from the lake and into a densely populated residential area.

The man didn't look like the sort who'd give up easily. In Hunter's experience, there were any number of reasons why someone would order him followed. The primary one, though, was that people didn't like it when you stole from them, even if what you were stealing was something they'd stolen in the first place.

He drove his motorcycle into a neighborhood, parked under a canopy of trees, and took the opportunity to text Mary he'd be late. Lights in the homes nearby were on, and children had gone inside for dinner—a quiet place where nothing out of the ordinary ever happened, and Hunter planned to keep it that way.

His plan was to ride around a while longer, distancing himself from this area, park his bike, and take a taxi to Mary's. The second text he sent was to the man who'd hired him for the Italy assignment. The text was short and to the point:

Someone is following me.

****

A few hours later, Hunter knocked on the door of Mary's home, a cozy three-bedroom overlooking Lake Sammamish. It had been in her family since the early nineteen-fifties, and she'd decorated the inside with antique furniture.

Hunter had received a response from his contact that they were looking into who might have had him followed. Hunter was doing the same on his end. His current assignment might not be connected to his tail. He'd made enemies over the years, and one of them could have resurfaced.

The front door opened, and a small replica of Mary's husband rushed to wrap his arms around

Hunter's legs as Mary greeted Hunter with a smile. Her three-year-old had a solid little body, coal-dark eyes, and curly hair.

Hunter laughed and picked him up. "Heh, Sir Rug-Rat. How's it going?"

"I drew a picture of Mama and Papa. Want to see?"

"You're my favorite painter. You know I do."

The boy squeezed Hunter's neck, then wiggled to be set down. According to Mary, her son, like his dad, was in constant motion.

"Thank you," Mary said. "You're so good with Bradley. As soon as he heard you were coming, he made John and me pose for our portrait."

Hunter watched her son scamper down the hallway to his bedroom. There was so much warmth and love in Mary's home. He remembered Lady Roselyn asking him if he were lonely.

He cleared his throat. "Your kid's talented. I meant it when I told him I liked his artwork. I can tell a genuine from a fake, but I can't draw or sculpt. My mum was the type of mother who tried to encourage me, saying things like my hands were too big or if I just practiced enough. But your kid's got it." Hunter lifted his head. "What smells so good? Is John barbequing?"

"You know he is. John was thrilled when you called and asked if you could come over for dinner. Something about you're the only one who appreciates his cooking. The moment the call ended, he headed to the butcher's shop to buy half a pig and a side of beef. I hope you're hungry. I'm trying to introduce more salads and vegetables into his life, but John only likes meat cooked over an open flame."

"My kind of guy. Not a fan of green food, and I'm

starving. John outside?"

"He's waiting for you." She paused. "About the question you asked me? I have to say I was surprised after our conversation this morning that you'd changed your mind and were interested in dating again."

Hunter had a flashback of the man in the sedan who'd followed him. "On second thought, maybe now's not the best time."

"Dating is always a good idea. Besides, it's already arranged. No turning back. Do you remember my telling you about my college friend Genevieve Grey? Well, she called me a short time after you called, and she asked for an introduction. Small world."

Genevieve's expression during her conversation with the man at her table sprang to Hunter's mind. At first, he'd thought it was a business meeting, but he'd seen hurt in her eyes and recognized it for what it was: personal betrayal. "She was with someone at the bakery," he said. "Let's call it one of your signs that I should back off and forget I called. On a more serious topic, my stomach is protesting, big time. I should find out how John's doing outside."

"Oh, you mean Frank Griffin. They work together at the *Daily Beat* newspaper. He's not important."

"Genevieve's a reporter?"

"Almost as good as you." Mary grinned. "Only she writes a column about bridezillas, self-absorbed celebrities, and exotic locations. You two have a lot in common."

"Hardly. Reporting on a wedding isn't dangerous."

"Most of the time you'd be right, but you haven't read her columns, have you? I never miss one. Last month Genevieve prevented a bride from shooting her husband when she learned he was cheating on her with the maid of honor."

"Impressive. Even so, I'm not interested."

"Excuse me if I don't believe you. You brought up the matchmaker sisters' company at breakfast, remember, and then called me asking if I could set you up with one of my single friends."

He rubbed the back of his neck. "What's keeping Rug-Rat? I thought he'd be right back."

"He has more than one picture he wants to show you, and you're changing the subject. You made quite an impression on Genevieve. She said the two of you had a conversation at the bakery. She hadn't realized you were *the* Hunter Longfellow. She said you were charming. Why didn't you tell me?"

"Charming? I plowed into her and spilled coffee over her suit. I doubt she'd say that I was charming. Besides, I said I was no longer interested. Why are you being so persistent?"

"You called me, remember? You and Genevieve are perfect for each other, and Nissa agrees. The sisters are saving a spot for the two of you on the tour."

"Who is Nissa?"

"She is one of the matchmaker sisters…well, their half-sister. She called right after you'd left and approached me with the idea. So when Genevieve phoned it felt like it was meant to be. But that is not the point. I don't know why I didn't think of the two of you on my own. And when Genevieve called right after your phone call, I knew it was a sign, regardless of how much fun you make of me when I say such a thing." Mary linked her arm in his and guided him to the back yard. "I arranged for the two of you to meet tomorrow morning, Village entrance, nine o'clock sharp. Now, let's see how John is doing. Don't tell him I said so, but the food he's barbequing smells amazing."

"That's high praise, coming from a vegetarian."

She laughed. "So true."

"You're enjoying being a matchmaker, aren't you?"

She grinned and pushed against him gently. "Like Christmas, New Year's, and the Fourth of July all rolled into one."

Chapter Ten

The next day, Genevieve stood in her compact kitchen and lined up the ingredients for what she called her Chocolate Therapy Breakfast. When she'd signed the lease for her place over five years ago, the advertisement had described it as the perfect one-bedroom, one-bath apartment for the up-and-coming executive. It featured a combination living room and kitchen area in hideous neutral tones. What had sold her on the apartment was the mountain view of the Cascade Range and the fact that it met her budget needs.

The moment she'd signed the papers, she'd redecorated with antiques and floral wallpaper until her tiny apartment resembled a set from her favorite series, *Downton Abbey*. Frank hated it. In contrast, his apartment was chrome and black leather. Definitely not her style. Funny, she'd never thought about it that way before. She only knew she'd never wanted to spend any length of time there.

She poured a cup of coffee and glanced over at the clock on the microwave. She should eat a healthy breakfast, but right now, she needed chocolate. It was six o'clock in the morning, and she'd been awake all night, researching Hunter Longfellow. She'd printed out all the articles he'd written, which amounted to a huge word count. She'd arranged them on her counter in neat stacks, by the countries in which the thefts had occurred, and then subdivided the stacks according to whether the art was stolen from a museum, an archeological site, or a private collector.

Genevieve had found only one biography of the man. It was posted by one of the New York newspapers he wrote for and was more a series of bullet points than an in-depth exposé. Longfellow had grown up on the Makah Indian reservation along the coast, his parents were deceased, he'd enlisted in the Air Force—flown helicopters in Afghanistan and been honorably discharged—and graduated from Eastern Washington University. He won a Pulitzer for his discovery and capture of thieves who had stolen artifacts from a Native American burial ground, and that led to stronger artifact protection laws. There was no mention of why he was interested in writing or in recovering stolen art.

She, on the other hand, had been born into the newspaper business and never considered any other profession. She loved the idea of sharing stories with those who read her columns. She knew Frank didn't believe what she wrote was important, and of late she was having doubts of her own.

She picked up a recent Longfellow article on the recovery of a painting by Caravaggio, painted in sixteen hundred and five. It depicted the Mother Mary teaching Baby Jesus how to defeat evil by showing him how to step on the head of a snake. According to Longfellow, the Church had refused the painting because they disliked the idea that Jesus had to be taught how to defeat evil. They believed he had been born with that knowledge. Longfellow believed the objection was not so much that Jesus was being taught how to defeat evil but that his teacher was a woman.

Genevieve sat on the edge of a stool and smoothed her hand over the paper she'd just read. Longfellow's articles always included a touch of history that wasn't common knowledge. She supposed that was the reason she, and countless others, were so drawn to them. There was more to what he wrote than a simple retelling of facts. He wrote with emotion. How did he do that? What was his story?

She shook her head, wondering if he'd ever let anyone get close enough to ask.

Genevieve reached for the ingredients for her breakfast, including dark chocolate, marshmallows, and pecans, and then tore open the bag of marshmallows.

The bag split, scattering them over the articles like plump snowflakes. She wondered if Longfellow would have thought it disrespectful that his pages were covered in sticky marshmallows. She shook her head. Probably, remembering his expression when he'd caught her in his arms at the bakery. His expression had been stoic. The man didn't have a funny bone in his body, regardless of how gorgeous and hard that body had looked and felt.

"Good grief," she said aloud as she reached for a marshmallow. "Where did that thought come from? You're engaged. You shouldn't be crushing on other men. Especially one that is the direct opposite of Frank." But what would it be like to be someone like Longfellow, who dropped everything at a moment's notice and set off on adventures? What would it be like to go with him? The thought sent an unexpected thrill of excitement down her back.

"Stop thinking about Hunter Longfellow in that way." She paused. Great. She was talking aloud to herself.

She stuffed her mouth with yet another marshmallow and started cutting the rest of them into quarters. They had no nutritional value whatsoever. The thought made her feel better. She'd always done everything by the book, as the saying went. What would it feel like to step outside her comfort zone? She could eat more marshmallows.

She broke up the dark chocolate candy bar into squares and put them into a large glass measuring pitcher, then into the microwave to heat. While the chocolate melted, she opened the bag of pre-chopped pecans. There was comfort in following the rules, but a little voice in the back of her thoughts had been awakened to a rebellious idea.

She heard a key turn in the lock and the door opened slightly.

"It's your mother. Can I come in?"

"I've been expecting you," Genevieve said over her shoulder as she opened the microwave and took out the liquefied chocolate. "I'm making enough for the both of us." She poured half the chocolate into a nine-by-nine glass square pan.

"I thought I smelled chocolate." Her mother joined her in the kitchen, dressed for work in a pastel blue suit that matched the shade of her eyes, and reached for one of the marshmallows on the counter. "I take it Frank's not here." She turned over one of the research papers on Hunter Longfellow.

"Frank was working late last night and thought it easier if he stayed at his own place." The words sounded rehearsed, as though she'd said some version of them countless times before.

Her mother only nodded and picked up one of the articles. "Frank was right about one thing. Hunter Longfellow has traveled to some pretty amazing places." She glanced toward Genevieve. "Why were you so sure I'd be here this morning?"

Genevieve sprinkled the chopped pecans and quartered marshmallows over the liquid chocolate and then reached into the refrigerator for a jar of maraschino cherries. "You always visit when I'm struggling with a decision."

Her mother sipped the coffee Genevieve had handed her. "Mother's intuition. What have you decided? Are you going on the matchmaker tour to Italy with Hunter Longfellow?"

"Frank wants me to go."

"That's not what I asked."

Genevieve added the cherries and drizzled the remainder of the chocolate over the ingredients in a crisscross design. "But even if I wanted to go, Longfellow might have already found someone to play the part of his girlfriend."

"Have you contacted him?"

Genevieve licked chocolate off her fingers. "Not exactly. I did call Mary last night and asked if she could arrange a meeting with Longfellow this morning at nine o'clock. She asked if I wanted to join them for dinner, but I made up an excuse. I lied and told her I'd broken off my engagement with Frank and wanted to start dating."

"Interesting. You lied about your relationship with Frank."

"What is that supposed to mean?"

"Nothing. Go on."

"Mary is a friend of mine from college. She's the one who knows Longfellow. That's why I called her."

"You're stalling, and you know very well that I know who Mary is. The two of you were like sisters. Question. Why do you refer to him by his last name only?"

"Am I?" Genevieve stared at the dessert she'd made. "I should put this breakfast-dessert in the refrigerator and wait until it hardens."

Her mother reached around and withdrew two spoons from the cutlery drawer. "Or we could eat it warm."

Genevieve smiled. "As my mother, shouldn't you be lecturing me on eating a healthy breakfast?"

"Perhaps, but as your boss, I believe in the fortification qualities of chocolate and how it helps the decision-making process."

"You made that up."

"Absolutely not. I read somewhere that dark chocolate is a brain food and has more antioxidants than blueberries. We'd be risking both our mental and our physical health if we *didn't* eat what you've made."

Genevieve laughed as she handed her mother a plate of warm chocolate. "I love you, Mom."

"And I love you to the moon and back." Her mother's spoon hovered over the dish. "You added cherries."

Genevieve scooped up a corner of the chocolate. "I wanted to try something new. What should I do about the trip with Longfellow? Should I go?"

Her mother shoved a generous helping of dessert onto her spoon. "Remember our newspaper motto is to find the heart of a story. What's in your heart?"

Chapter Eleven

The next morning, Hunter waited in the parking lot near the Village entrance. The weather gods had opted to give Seattleites a break from the rain and had tossed in the makings of a sunny day. Hunter felt it was by design. Just when people in the Pacific Northwest had had enough of the gray days, the weather turned, reminding them that there were few places on earth as spectacular. Any other day, he'd seize the opportunity to hop on his bike and ride until the tension in his shoulders eased. Meeting with Genevieve Grey was a bad idea.

He couldn't blame Mary for arranging this with Genevieve. He'd asked Mary to set him up with one of her single friends. Of course, his reasoning had been to ask one of them if she would be interested in posing as his girlfriend for seven days. Not the Richard Gere-Julia Roberts-style arrangement in the movie *Pretty Woman*, of course. Hunter's proposal was one hundred percent platonic—no sex and no romance. He'd pay generously for the woman's time and provide an open-ended, first-class return ticket if she had a change of mind.

Being followed last night had changed everything. He didn't want to bring an inexperienced person on an assignment that could go sideways and potentially get them hurt. His contact felt confident that the man who'd followed Hunter last night wasn't connected to the current assignment. Hunter wasn't convinced.

He checked his watch. He'd tried to convince Mary to cancel the meeting with Genevieve but couldn't give her the real reason for his change of heart. All his excuses had sounded lame. Mary said he'd have to face Genevieve himself.

The good news was that all Genevieve knew was that he was interested in dating. When he saw her, he'd tell her he'd changed his mind, or was in a bad place, or it wasn't her, it was him. The standard excuses.

He leaned against his Harley. This was a bad idea, he repeated to himself.

He shifted his weight. No matter how many times he told himself he wasn't attracted to Genevieve and those eyes of hers that seemed to see into his soul, he knew he was kidding himself. At the bakery when Mocha had jumped on him and he'd plowed into Genevieve, she'd fallen into his arms as naturally as if there'd been a grand design in play. She fit against his body as though they were two halves of the same whole. He hadn't wanted to let her go. Even without the incident last night, he'd have had to abandon his plan to ask her to pretend to be his girlfriend on this assignment, if only out of self-preservation.

Mary had arranged for him and Genevieve to meet at nine a.m. at the Village entrance. He'd arrived early. Last night he'd researched the matchmaker sisters. There wasn't much beyond the story Genevieve had written in the *Daily Beat*. They'd apparently sprouted fully grown as though from thin air, which brought up a red flag. Especially for people who displayed priceless works of art and passed them off as family heirlooms.

The Scheherazade portrait supposedly created or acquired by Lady Roselyn's ancestor wasn't the only item that had caught Hunter's attention. Lady Roselyn's diamond brooch with the heart-shaped ruby had once appeared in a portrait of Marie Antoinette, a gift from her lover.

The moment he'd left the Matchmaker Café, he knew he'd investigate the tip from his unknown source. He thrived on solving mysteries, and this one had all the elements he loved: stolen art, people who weren't who they said they were, exotic locations, and the threat of danger.

He glanced at his watch yet again, realizing that for a man who was always running late, he was suddenly obsessed with time. It was eight forty-five a.m. Fifteen minutes to go. If she didn't show, maybe he'd have time for that ride after all.

A few cars drove into the parking lot. All were the family-style SUV variety, many with cartoon decals representing the number of family members on the rear window. Some even had cartoon dogs or cats, and one set of decals were Star Wars characters. As more cars entered, Hunter wondered what make of car Genevieve drove. She dressed like a fashion model, so he guessed sports car or expensive electric hybrid. Probably red to reflect a fire he suspected she hid, or emerald green, the color of her eyes. He ground his teeth together.

Why did he have to start thinking about the type of car she drove—or anything about her, for that matter? After today he'd never see her again. Telling himself not to think about her, however, was backfiring. He couldn't stop thinking about her. He remembered her expression when she was petting Mocha. Yesterday her expression had reminded him of the painting of the Mona Lisa. Today he figured the likeness would be closer to Da Vinci's portrait *Lady with an Ermine*. Bad sign that he was comparing Genevieve to paintings. It was common knowledge that many of the Italian masters painted portraits of women they knew would never love them.

A red Tesla, bicyclers, and another SUV drove into the parking lot. Nine o'clock sharp.

She hadn't come after all. Could be she'd changed her mind or was still putting on makeup. Either way, he'd figure out another way onto the matchmaker tour. He reached for his helmet, burying the sudden jolt of disappointment.

"Hi."

Hunter spun around in response to the decidedly feminine voice.

Genevieve was a few feet away, walking toward him. She wore faded jeans and a green pullover sweater a shade lighter than her eyes. Her hair was pulled back into a long ponytail, and a bicycle helmet dangled from a strap on her fingers. Her cheeks were flushed, and her eyes sparkled. For a split second he wondered if she'd like to have coffee with him, or lunch at the family restaurant in the Village, dinner at the Bistro, or his place…

He clamped his teeth together. Focus. Genevieve believes she's meeting you here because you're interested in a date. But you're here to tell her that Mary's phone call was a mistake, and after you list off your excuses, you'll confirm Genevieve's first impression that you're a jerk.

"Hi," he said as she drew closer. He yanked out of

59

his fog with a mental shake, remembering the cyclists who'd ridden into the parking lot a few minutes ago. She must have been one of them. That she'd ridden her bike to their meeting, not driven an expensive car, made him glad for reasons he didn't want to examine too closely.

"You rode your bike here?" he said, stating the obvious, then cringed.

"It was a beautiful morning," she said, her words tumbling out in a rush. "I thought it a waste to drive. Plus, I'm not going in to work today. I have to start packing." She took in a sharp breath. "I'll go with you on the trip as your girlfriend. Strictly business, separate bedrooms."

He dropped his helmet and bent to retrieve it from the ground. "How do you know about the trip?"

She also bent to retrieve his helmet, and as they bumped heads, she rolled back on her heels.

He reached for her before she fell.

"Sorry," she said as she rubbed her forehead and gave him a smile that threatened to stop his heart mid-beat. "We seem to always be bumping into each other. Do you think that's a sign?"

He kept stone still. Of course he believed it was a sign. He was Native American. His people believed in that sort of thing and studied signs morning, noon, and night, and right now he didn't like what the signs were shouting. "You were about to tell me about a trip you think I'm going on."

"I was in the Matchmaker Café and overheard you talking to Bridget. You need a girlfriend, and I want in on whatever story you're investigating."

The expression of the man following him last night

flashed like a police mug shot. "I changed my mind. There's no story."

"And you are a very bad liar."

"Excuse me?"

She shifted her weight, much as he had moments before. "I don't believe you. Everything I've learned about you supports the conclusion that you're like a dog digging for a bone once you are onto a story. You don't give up. You wanted to be part of the Italy tour. I don't buy that you changed your mind."

He let the reference to her investigating him slide. Partly because it irritated him and partly because he was impressed. "Dog digging for a bone? That's a pretty old cliché."

She perched her hand on her hip. "I'm sorry. Should I wax more literary, Mr. Pulitzer Prize? If you don't want me along, say so. Don't, however, tell me you've changed your mind about a story."

"What if I told you it's too dangerous?"

She hesitated, and a shadow clouded those lovely green eyes for an instant, then disappeared. "I can do danger."

"No."

She lifted an eyebrow. "Yes, or I will tell the sisters that I suspect they are under investigation or you wouldn't be finagling to go on this tour, and that will blow your assignment."

"You wouldn't do that."

"And you don't know me." She handed him a card. "My address is on the back. When we make the arrangements with the sisters, you can pick me up at my home. We should go together. It will look more convincing."

He turned the card over. Her handwriting was neat and tidy. He knew his looked like Egyptian hieroglyphics. "Are you always this pushy?"

Her expression faltered as though it might crack. "I have to go on this assignment. Please don't say no." She hesitated and glanced away. "I thought because you agreed to meet with me that you hadn't found anyone else. Are you still looking for a girlfriend?"

"Mary seems to think I need one. But no, I'm not looking for a girlfriend."

"I mean…for the Italy tour."

"I knew what you meant." Her vulnerability took him off guard. He changed the subject. "Do you ride your bike often?"

"Not as much as I'd like," she said. "You probably want to know a little about me. I'm also a reporter—nothing like you, but someday perhaps. Anyway, I write a column on celebrity engagements and weddings for the *Daily Beat*. We syndicate your column, and as you know from my embarrassing display when I bumped into you with my umbrella, I'm a huge fan. That's why when I overheard you trying to sign up for the Italy tour, I knew you were working on a story. Full disclosure…it wasn't my idea to ask you if I could go along. It was my fiancé's."

It felt as though a cloud had smothered the sun. "You're engaged?"

Hunter remembered the man she had been with at the bakery but hadn't thought they were a couple. The man had spent too much time checking his messages or checking out every pretty woman who passed near his table. How could any man not give Genevieve his full attention? "Does Mary know?"

She nodded again. "Mary knew about Frank. I think the world knew. I bragged about how he proposed in one of my columns. I exaggerated a little about the romance of how it happened, but I'm a wedding columnist, and my readers expected that sort of thing from me. The truth is I don't even have an engagement ring. Frank proposed in a text and said he planned to ask his mother for his grandmother's ring…someday." She looked away. "Frank told me I should let Mary know that we'd called off our engagement. Like I said, this is his idea."

"What about you?"

"At first I wasn't sure."

"What changed your mind?"

There was that long hesitation again. Just when he thought she hadn't heard him, she turned toward him with a smile. Not the warm kind that lit up her face but something more thoughtful, wistful. "It was something you said in one of your articles. It's time for a change. I can pretend to be your girlfriend, and you can teach me how to be an investigative reporter by letting me come along. You're investigating a story and I want to be part of it."

"You might not, if you knew what it was."

"Try me."

He hesitated. Could he trust her to keep what he'd told her a secret? He'd investigated her as well and knew the answer. It was true that she wrote a gossip column, but also true was the fact that if a client wanted her to keep something a secret, she would.

"I suspect the sisters are stealing art." He watched the play of emotions over her expression. Surprise. Shock. Disappointment. And then the one that told him she was a reporter: curiosity.

She raised her chin. "Should you let the sisters know you can go on the Italy trip after all, or should we go in together?"

Chapter Twelve

Lady Roselyn shut the door to her bedroom and leaned against the red rosebuds on the wallpaper. She should feel pleased. They'd just booked their final couple on the matchmaking tour to Italy: Genevieve and Hunter. The truth was that Nissa knew all along it would be Genevieve and Hunter. And if Nissa was anything like Fiona, Lady Roselyn was sure Nissa had worked her magic to get Genevieve and Hunter together.

Regardless of all the good news, Lady Roselyn was on edge. Claude had appeared out of nowhere, asked for her forgiveness, and had given her a cameo brooch as a peace offering. Her sisters thought he might be sincere. Lady Roselyn wasn't as sure.

She pushed off from the wall and unbuttoned her blouse at the neck. Her collar was too tight. Her sisters dressed more casually, but she felt it was important to dress in the style of a matronly matchmaker from the nineteenth century, which made her look—and at times feel—decades older than her actual age. Usually it didn't bother her, but of late everything bothered her. The least of which was that the doors weren't working as intended. It had been the reason they'd created the Italy tour.

The situation with Emma and Björn had been the perfect example. To jog them out of the "friend zone," the sisters had planned to have Emma and Björn use a door to time travel them back to eighteen eighty-nine in Paris, for a romantic interlude during the opening of the Moulin Rouge. Instead, they'd been sent back in time to the eve of the French Revolution in seventeen eighty-nine. A hundred-year difference and a whole lot more dangerous.

She crossed the room, trying to calm her nerves. She'd had her bedroom decorated to reflect Jane Austen's world. Wallpaper with tiny tea rosebuds and matching bedcovers set a mood of tranquility. A four-poster bed made from mahogany and an antique wardrobe that reminded her of a book from the Narnia series, *The Lion, the Witch and the Wardrobe*, completed the picture.

The similarities between her favorite series as a child and how she and her sisters created time-travel adventures for their couples hadn't escaped Lady Roselyn's notice. The children in the Narnia series opened the wardrobe doors and were transported to a fantasy world. The sisters used a system of enchanted doors to accomplish a similar goal. But that was only the beginning of the likeness. Their theory was that without the stress and distractions of day-to-day life, people had the chance to discover their strengths, desires, and dreams. That was the real magic of the doors.

Her room had been a retreat, a touchstone to remind her that, like in Jane's stories, there was always a happy ending. When had she stopped believing?

She heard a knock on the door as soft as down and knew immediately it was her half-sister, Nissa.

"Come in, the door's unlocked."

The door opened silently. "Bridget needs you."

Nissa's words were like a cold shower, waking her from self-reflection. Bridget needed her. "Lead the way."

She rushed after Nissa to the third floor and Bridget's bedroom. If Lady Roselyn's bedroom reflected the romance of Jane Austen, Bridget's belonged to an ice-princess, all white and glacial blue, like Elsa had created in the movie *Frozen*. Even though Bridget's bedroom was a comfortable temperature, Lady Roselyn shivered. Bridget's room reflected her desire to keep everyone at a distance.

Nissa went in ahead of Lady Roselyn, as silent as mist, and perched on Bridget's foam-white bed, watching Bridget pack for her trip to Italy. Bridget was scheduled to arrive before the tour group to assure that everything would go as planned.

Bridget glanced toward Lady Roselyn: a tremor caused her words to shake. "I have a problem. I need a bigger suitcase."

Lady Roselyn's concern grew. This wasn't like Bridget. Not only was Bridget the most self-reliant sister, she was also the one who packed light. Lady Roselyn noticed that Bridget had packed boxes of chocolate truffles, candy bars, and Oreo cookies into her suitcase instead of clothes. She and her sisters joked that chocolate was the miracle food that cured everything from the common cold to heartbreak, but this was over the top, even for them.

"We have a steamer trunk in the attic," Lady Roselyn said, trying to lighten the mood. "Would you like me to call for a taxi? Your flight leaves in a few hours."

Bridget wedged a box of chocolate wafers into a side pocket of the suitcase. "Good idea about the steamer trunk. Do you think William could bring it down for me?"

Lady Roselyn pressed her hand against her stomach as her concern spiked. Bridget hadn't picked up on the joke.

Nissa glanced toward Lady Roselyn as though asking permission to speak.

Lady Roselyn nodded slightly and mouthed a silent thank you. Nissa was petite, barely five feet tall, her pixie-cut the color of wheat, just long enough to cover her ears. The shade of her eyes varied from the ocean at night to the green of a spring forest. What Lady Roselyn knew of Nissa only conjured more questions than answers. Nissa had been born before Lady Roselyn and yet looked younger than Fiona. Their mother had never mentioned the identity of Nissa's father, but he was rumored to be Oberon, King of the Fairies.

Nissa smiled as though she'd read Lady Roselyn's thoughts and reached out toward Bridget, resting her hand over hers. "You do not need more chocolate. You have everything you need. I promise."

"What if the tour group gets lost?" Bridget said, sitting down on the bed beside Nissa. "Or instead of the couples rekindling their love, they grow further apart? I've never been in complete charge of a couple on a romantic adventure, let alone a tour group. What if I fail?"

Lady Roselyn rushed to the bed, chiding herself for not realizing Bridget's worry sooner. "You won't fail. You will be a wonderful matchmaker."

Nissa took both of Bridget's hands in hers. "Lady

Roselyn is right. You're a matchmaker. You won't fail. My wish is that you open your heart, dear sister, and know that you are not alone." Nissa jumped off the bed and opened a dresser drawer, pulling out a stack of sweaters. "Lady Roselyn will order a taxi, and I'll help you finish packing. I suggest a seventy-thirty split. Seventy percent clothes, and thirty percent chocolate."

Bridget blinked away the tears that had filled her eyes and sniffled. "I can live with that."

Chapter Thirteen

Three days later, Hunter adjusted the backpack on his shoulder as he waited beside the limo that would take Genevieve and him to the airport. He'd happily have ridden the bus into Seattle, but he guessed Genevieve was not the bus kind of gal. Actually, he didn't know what she was really like. She'd ridden a bicycle to their meeting, so it was a high possibility that he hadn't a clue about her.

Which made what he was doing insane. He'd considered backing out and finding another way to investigate whether the matchmaker sisters were running a theft ring, but all the plans he'd come up with weren't as good as this one. He and Genevieve would pretend to be girlfriend and boyfriend on the sisters' Italy tour while they gathered evidence.

Genevieve walked out of the apartment building, pulling a suitcase that looked big enough to carry a body. She wore a figure-hugging sleeveless white dress and four-inch heels. It was a ten-hour flight to London and another five, counting the layover, to Rome. He'd opted for comfort, wearing jeans and a T-shirt. He disagreed with her choice but admitted he enjoyed the view. Genevieve was a fine-looking woman. Down, boy, he cautioned. Remember the last time you fell for a pretty face? Armageddon.

He went over to help her with her luggage, but she

shook off his help.

"You know we're just going for a week, right?" he said.

"My mother helped me pack. It was her final condition."

"She had others?"

Genevieve allowed the limo driver to haul her luggage into the trunk. "My mother gave me a two-page, double-spaced list and made me sign it." The limo driver opened the door, and Genevieve slid in. "You were on the list."

"As a do, or as a don't?"

She scooted further away from him and hugged the window. "She didn't say."

Chapter Fourteen

Lady Roselyn paced inside the Matchmaker Café. It had been days since she and Nissa had taken Bridget to the airport and hugged their goodbyes. She'd had one communication from Bridget when she'd arrived. Since then, not a bloody word. Had all the hotel and museum arrangements been made? Had she overdosed on chocolate?

In the main room of the Matchmaker Café there was a constant stream of customers who came inside to learn more about the sisters' success at finding a person's soulmate. But in the back of the café, things were not as hopeful, and Lady Roselyn was losing patience.

"Why won't this door open? William? Where are you?" She kept an eye on the customers. Even though Nissa had everything under control, and they were busier than they'd ever been, she felt a premonition that her world was about to crumble at her feet. What if they never got the enchanted doors to work again? Would they have to resort to online matchmaking?

She stepped back from the door she'd been trying to open, perched her hands on her hips, and shouted again, "William!"

William appeared next to her, out of breath. "Is something wrong?" He reminded her of a middle-aged Sean Connery, gray hair at his temples, an easy smile and a glint in his eyes that sent her heart racing.

"I haven't heard from Bridget in days," she said, ordering her heart rate under control. "Which is very unlike her. Disappearing without a word is more Fiona's thing, and I can't open this door, which is strange, because it's not a time-travel door: it's one that can take me someplace in this time. I'm worried about Bridget. I thought if I popped over to Rome…"

"You could take a plane."

She frowned. "Not funny. You know I hate to fly. I need to find out if she arrived in Rome safely and to check on the progress of the tour, but this door won't open."

William slipped his hands into hers and squeezed gently.

Her skin warmed at his touch. "What are you doing?" she whispered.

"My gal is stressed. I'm lending my support."

She removed her hands from his, glancing around to see if anyone had noticed the exchange. "That's not helping. No one is supposed to…" She cleared her throat. "I have to focus, and you haven't answered my question."

"It's not the only door that won't open," William said evenly.

"I need to sit down."

William fetched her a chair, then knelt beside her. "Nissa seems to be working out."

Lady Roselyn let out a short, clipped laugh. "Changing the subject?" She laughed again. "But what if Nissa gets excited, or frightened, or stressed? Her fairy wings might pop out unexpectedly and startle the clients."

William chuckled. "I'm not sure that's how it works with fairy wings, or even if the rumors about her father being the King of the Fairies are true. Have you asked her?"

"The question feels too personal." Lady Roselyn took a long, even breath. "Thank you. Changing the subject helped. But what are we going to do about the doors?"

"I'm the Keeper of the Doors for a reason. It's true many won't open, or if they do, they open on the wrong date or century."

"Do you believe this problem will spread?"

"It's hard to know for sure or even to know when the problem first started. I've contacted one of our Timekeepers to meet with us. I thought it best, however, not to tell him the reason. They tend to overreact when it comes to these sorts of things. If it were up to them, they'd forbid us to time travel."

"The last thing we need are more people involved."

"Agreed. But Duncan MacAlpin is not just anyone. I trust him."

When Lady Roselyn had gone back in time to Paris during the French Revolution, to help rescue Emma and Björn, she'd learned that her husband was still alive. She'd thought Claude might be responsible for the doors not opening to the dates in time as they'd been programmed. Now she wasn't sure it was that simple. The date mix-up could be an accident. No one knew for certain how long the doors had been enchanted. Maybe, like a car's engine, they were wearing out and unreliable. That was why she'd told Bridget that under no circumstances was she to use a door to travel back in time.

"When does Duncan MacAlpin arrive?" she said.
"Any minute."

****

Lady Roselyn stood in front of the oak door that dated back to the Crusades. William had installed it in the attic of the café to prevent anyone from seeing the Timekeeper arrive. William stood by the entrance to the attic, keeping guard. The fewer people who knew about this door and their plan, the better. She feared Nissa might want to talk them out of the unprecedented idea of sending a Timekeeper on a matchmaking experience while it was in progress.

Timekeepers were the fixers, the ones who came in after a matchmaker tour or a couple adventure and made sure events in history weren't changed. They also did not believe in love and adhered to a monastic way of life, which meant no long-term relationships and no family. Their life philosophy and dedication to keeping time in balance meant that they didn't approve of matchmakers using time travel to help couples find love. They were chosen because of their commitment to duty and their clinical view that love was an illusion.

Lady Roselyn believed the opposite—time was the illusion and love the only reality.

Mist rolled under the door, signaling that someone was coming through. The temperature dropped as the door opened. Duncan MacAlpin stood framed in the doorway, shirtless, arms folded, wearing only a green and black tartan plaid and a scowl. Sweat glistened on his chest and arms as though William had interrupted a training session when he'd summoned the man, or perhaps it was from some other form of entertainment. She hoped it was the latter. It would suggest he was human, which was a hotly contested debate amongst the matchmaking community.

She understood the man's appeal. He had long dark hair that grazed his bare shoulders, eyes the color of black granite, and a chiseled chin that would make famous actors envious. Any woman with a pulse would take a long second look at this hunk.

"Why was I summoned?" Duncan roared, sounding like the ruler of a small kingdom.

The fantasy bubble burst. The guy had an oversized ego to match his biceps.

Lady Roselyn squared her shoulders, praying this wasn't going to be a hard sell. "We need you to accompany my sister Bridget on a matchmaking tour. It's been underway for a few days, but I'll give you their itinerary."

"Bridget McBride?" His tone softened. "Bridget's your sister?" When Lady Roselyn nodded, he crossed over the threshold and closed the door. "I've met her a few times when she brought me the reports of your time-travel adventures. She never expressed a wish about conducting one herself."

Lady Roselyn recognized the change in Duncan's demeanor with the mention of Bridget's name. He'd said her name like a caress. Funny that her sister hadn't mentioned him. Well, well, the man had a heart after all. If she were a betting woman, she'd wager all the chocolate in the café that Duncan MacAlpin was smitten with Bridget. Lady Roselyn wondered if Bridget was aware of the man's interest.

She hid her excitement behind a serious tone. William had said he hadn't told Duncan the reason for his summons. She chose her words carefully. "We've created a new matchmaking experience for our couples—a matchmaking tour to Italy. Bridget agreed to be our first tour guide. Although it is a conventional tour, I'm worried. We haven't heard from her since she left." She cleared her throat. "We'd like you to check on her."

"A Timekeeper is not a babysitter. We go in *after* matchmakers. Why don't you open a door to her location?"

Lady Roselyn exchanged a worried glance with William.

"We cannot," he said. "The enchanted doors aren't as reliable as we'd like, so Bridget and the tour used a conventional mode of travel and flew to Rome. But we're worried that when she landed she may have opened the wrong door and is lost somewhere back in time. 'Tis the reason I summoned you." He glanced over toward Lady Roselyn again. "No one outside this room is to know."

Duncan narrowed his gaze. "So the rumors are true." He crossed over to the window, hands behind his back. The muscles across his shoulders tightened. "We've been worried about this scenario for centuries. People touching things in the past and interacting with the indigenous surroundings would be a nightmare."

Lady Roselyn felt her frustration grow. She and William were asking for help not judgment. "Bridget is a professional. She will make sure no one touches anything."

Duncan turned to face her. "I meant no disrespect, and you're right, Bridget is one of the most conscientious people I've ever met. I leave at once."

Chapter Fifteen

Genevieve stood in the baggage claim line at the Leonardo da Vinci International Airport. She had arrived in Rome. Her luggage had not. She also hadn't a clue what had happened to Hunter. She knew, however, the exact moment she'd lost track of him. They'd boarded the plane in Seattle together. She'd turned right to find her coach seat, and he'd turned left into first-class after mumbling something about air miles.

She clutched her tote to her chest as she inched forward. She doubted first-class passengers worried about lost luggage.

Announcements for departures and arrivals rolled out in a robotic voice, and when a departure flight came for the U.S., Genevieve seriously considered bailing from the line and sprinting over to the escalator that would take her upstairs to purchase a return ticket.

The biggest difference between this airport and others she'd experienced was the sound. Everything was louder—the roll of luggage across the floor, conversations, crowds. In addition, no one warned you in the guidebooks that Italians cut in line. As a result, it was taking three times as long for Genevieve to reach the counter of the Customer Service Desk.

She dialed her mother's cell phone number and then looked at the time. It was noon in Rome, which would make it three in the morning Seattle time. Before she could end the call, her mother picked up with a groggy, "Genevieve, is everything okay?"

Guilt swamped Genevieve. She didn't want to worry her mother, and what would be gained by complaining like a spoiled ten-year-old that her luggage was lost? Did she expect her mother to swoop down and rescue her?

"Mother, I'm fine, and everything is better than expected. I forgot about the time difference. Please, go back to sleep, and I'll talk to you later."

Her mother mumbled, "I love you," and ended the call.

Genevieve moved forward another inch in the line. She knew if she had complained, her mother would hop on the next flight to Rome, launch an investigation, and threaten to write a scathing article about airline inefficiencies. Genevieve smiled. That might be worth watching.

Even without the luggage incident, the airport in Rome was disappointing. She'd expected more romance, more music, more pasta restaurants, and perhaps a slower pace. Maybe she'd watched the movie *Under the Tuscan Sun* too many times and that had clouded her opinion. She really had thought that once she reached Italy she'd have the urge to buy a villa. True, she was in an airport, but still…

Why had she thought she could do this?

The feel of Hunter when he'd caught her in his strong arms in the bakery and held her against him as she gazed into eyes that could melt a glacier flooded back. Hunter had asked her what had changed her mind about the trip, and she'd said it had to do with something he'd said in one of his articles. That had been one of the tallest tales she'd ever told. She was surprised her nose, much like Pinocchio's, hadn't grown two feet long.

The truth was she didn't know what had changed her mind.

She finally reached the counter, handed the customer service woman the ticket with the tracking number, and recited the lines she'd rehearsed. "My luggage was not at the baggage claim area. Do you have any idea when it might arrive?" Genevieve hugged her tote bag against her chest as though it were a life preserver.

The woman behind the counter checked the number and started typing on her computer. "Your luggage was oversized and didn't make the last connection. We expect it will arrive soon," she added in the same robotic-sounding voice that blared over the airport's announcement system, and then added a perfect smile and a flip of her perfect hair.

The crack about the oversized luggage made Genevieve consider writing a scathing editorial about her experience. The customer service woman's comment and the I-couldn't-care-less-about-your-lost-luggage expression brought Genevieve to the tipping point.

Genevieve rested her arms on the counter. "You don't understand. I've signed up for a tour and I need my luggage. I bought this cute little black dress, slacks." She lowered her voice. "Lingerie… My luggage can't be lost. I can't wear what I'm wearing for seven days."

"I never check my luggage," the customer service woman said, "but if I do, I bring a change of clothes on the plane with me."

Genevieve resisted the impulse to reach across the counter and strangle the woman. Genevieve took a calming breath, knowing that would not end well. Maybe the woman with the perfect hair and skin thought her advice was helpful, not judgmental. "I'll keep that in mind."

The woman handed Genevieve an envelope and said the obvious. "Your luggage was not on the plane. Fill out these lost luggage forms, and when your suitcase arrives, we will deliver it to your hotel." She reached under the counter and produced a plastic pouch. "This contains toiletries and a night shirt, compliments of our airline. When you fill out the lost luggage form, please include the name of the tour and hotel where you'll be staying."

Genevieve fished in her tote bag and withdrew the folder with her itinerary. Everything was there. Being a control freak had its advantages. "I'm traveling with the Matchmaker Tour group, and we're staying at the Luna Hotel the first night. It overlooks a beach, and I brought this barely-there bikini…"

"Bikini?" a man said, and she knew the rich deep voice belonged to Hunter. "Are you sure you need one? Italy is famous for its nude beaches."

Her face warmed to what she could only imagine was flame-red. She didn't want to turn and face him. She wanted to run and hide. "They lost my luggage."

The woman behind the counter transformed. She stood up straighter, lifting her chest and batting thick eyelashes. "I assure you that we are doing our best to locate Miss Grey's luggage. Are the two of you staying together at the Luna Hotel in Rome?"

Hunter took the baggage claim from Genevieve and nodded toward the woman. "Our plans changed. We'll let you know where we're staying."

Genevieve jogged to keep pace with Hunter as he raced past the luggage carrousel to the exit.

"What do you mean our plans changed? I thought we were staying at the Luna Hotel. I'll have to let the airline know where to send my luggage."

He paused in front of the exit sign. "Your luggage is long gone. I put something in it as a test, and it worked. They took the bait…and your luggage."

"What are you talking about? Who took the bait?"

"That part I'm still working out, but when I loaded your luggage into the limo I slipped in a computer and our tour's itinerary."

"I'm not getting my luggage back, am I?"

He shook his head.

"Wait. How big was the computer you put in my suitcase? I had to sit on it to get it to closed."

"I may have taken out a few items. Most of your clothes were boring. I did find these that looked promising." He held up a bikini bottom and black lace panties and matching lace bra.

She snatched them out of his hand, knowing her blush was back with a vengeance, and as she fumbled to open her tote, it flipped over and the contents spilled onto the ground, scattering papers, cosmetics, pens, and a stash of dark chocolate. She stared over the mess, her vision blurring as she watched her favorite lip gloss roll away.

Hunter bent down to help and handed her the chocolate bar. "This candy bar is ninety percent dark chocolate. Isn't it bitter?"

She scooped up the rest of her treasures. "It suits my personality." She stuffed the candy bar into her tote and scanned to see if everything was there. Instead of all her things placed in neat little side pockets, they were stuffed together like her mother's kitchen junk drawer.

She closed her eyes for a second to calm her racing pulse. When she opened them, he was still staring at her. "We're supposed to be a couple. That means traveling together. How does it look if we arrive separately?"

"Like we're having problems and a perfect match for this tour. The bus is waiting for us in a no-loading zone. I volunteered to find you." He reached for her tote. "Can I carry that for you?"

She turned away from him. "You said my clothes were boring."

"Not everything." His grin was disarming.

She felt her face flush as she walked beside him toward the exit. When was the last time she'd blushed? College? No, it was middle school. "I'll have you know that my clothes are all vintage designer labels."

He shrugged. "They don't suit you."

Chapter Sixteen

What, for the love of chocolate, did Hunter mean when he said her clothes didn't suit her? What did a guy who looked like he had worn the same jeans and T-shirt since she'd met him know about fashion?

Hunter held the door open for her as she walked from the air-conditioned airport into the warmth of a Roman sun. A blast of heat pushed against her as she shielded her eyes from the bright sunlight. Horns honked as people labored with their suitcases, rushed to taxis and buses, or hailed friends and relatives. Waiting alongside the curb was a black, fifty-passenger tour bus with the words Matchmaker Tours splashed in green and white across its sides.

Genevieve heard her name and Hunter's shouted over the hum of traffic. Bridget was handing out bottles of water at the bus and waved to Genevieve and Hunter to hurry. Bridget's blonde hair was piled topsy-turvy on top of her head, but even in her cream-colored dress over matching leggings she seemed cool and fresh, as though the temperature were a comfortable seventy-five degrees instead of a scorching eighty-eight.

"Please tell me the bus is air-conditioned," Genevieve said more to herself than to Hunter.

"You can turn back," Hunter said, keeping pace with her. "Remember when I said this assignment might be dangerous? Stolen luggage was a reminder."

"Are you sure that's what happened?"

"Sure enough."

His presence was like her conscience, or maybe her protector, both intriguing and annoying. Could she turn back? Would it be that easy to board the next plane home? As a gossip columnist, she'd learned how to spin a story. She could tell her mother and her coworkers that the whole idea of the Matchmaker Tours being a front for an antiquities theft ring was a dead end. But if Hunter's allegations were right… She groaned as her cell phone rang out somewhere in the bottom of her tote bag.

She rummaged around and found her phone on the fourth ring, recognizing Frank's number.

"Hello, Frank." She listened as he said he hadn't heard from her and was just checking in to see if she'd arrived okay. He went on to promise that he'd look after her mother and the newspaper while she was gone. Both comments caused a rise in her temperature. She gripped the phone, rationalizing that he was trying to help. There was a long pause on Frank's end, and she knew it was her turn to respond. She looked over at Hunter. He'd accepted a bottle of water from Bridget, and although he was drinking, she knew he was listening in on her conversation.

"Thank you for looking after my mother and the newspaper," Genevieve said. "Yes, I had a very uneventful flight. The bus is here, though, so I should get going. Yes, I'll be sure to check in from time to time." She ended the call, realizing neither of them had said I love you.

Hunter handed her a bottle of water. "Uneventful flight? Why didn't you tell him about your lost luggage?"

"I didn't want to worry him, and he might have felt he had to take the next flight out and rescue me."

Hunter finished his water and recapped the bottle before tossing it into a waste receptacle. "Seriously? He doesn't seem the rescuing type, but you know him better than I do. Did you decide to return to Seattle?"

A breeze had the nerve to brush aside his long hair, exposing a jawline that would make Chris Pine jealous. She'd just finished talking to her fiancé. She shouldn't be staring at a man as though he were a chocolate sundae with extra sprinkles. If she were smart, she'd take the next plane bound for Seattle. Hunter was giving her a way out. Frank would be glad not to feel the need to watch over both her mother and the newspaper. Everybody won. Everybody but her, that was. She'd have given up before she even got the chance to find out if she had what it took to be an investigative reporter.

She squared her shoulders. "I told you we're in this together. I won't back out."

"Good to know."

She brushed past him, climbed onto the bus, and felt like she'd walked into an oven. Worst fears confirmed. No air-conditioning.

Bridget stood near the driver's seat, her smile warm and welcoming. "It's cooler in the back of the bus."

Genevieve nodded her thanks and headed toward a vacant seat, smiling hello to familiar faces. Gigi, Mr. Digby, Daisy, and Jorvy had joined the tour. The only couple Genevieve didn't recognize were seated near the back, huddled together reading over brochures.

"We're all here," Bridget said over the bus's P.A. system. "Everyone, please take your seats. We have a large bus, so feel free to stretch out. We'll be underway in a few minutes. We're parked in a no-loading zone and have been asked to leave. We also have a change in schedule. The hotel isn't ready for us yet, so we've had to make a few adjustments. We'll take in a museum first before checking into our hotel. No worries. I brought lots of chocolate and cookies."

Everyone on the bus cheered as though desserts solved everything.

The bus doors closed, and in the next instant it lurched forward, sending Genevieve into the nearest seat. She scrambled to right herself and slid toward the window, where she could see waves of heat rising from the street outside as the bus sped away from the airport toward the freeway. The tour was officially underway.

She glanced over her shoulder, knowing Hunter was in the seat behind her. He was poring over a leather-bound book as studiously as a college professor. She couldn't figure him out. She knew with a woman's instinct that he was the protector type. His strength and confidence were palpable, and yet, like now, she'd glimpsed another side to him.

She turned back in her seat and concentrated on Rome's mix of old world and new. "What have I gotten myself into?" she said under her breath.

Chapter Seventeen

The Matchmaker Café seemed to sigh in contentment under the warmth of the late afternoon sun. A fragrant summer breeze whispered through the trees, and the meandering creek nearby burbled that all was well.

Lady Roselyn inhaled the contentment as she filed the last of the tour brochures away and fingered the small gift box in the pocket of her skirt. Should she give it to him today? She'd spent most of her life looking over her shoulder, and today she wanted to cast that worry aside. William's plan to summon Duncan to help Bridget and the tour had been genius. Duncan had reported that except for the tour group experiencing jet lag, and the airline losing Genevieve Grey's luggage, everyone was having a great time.

William was arranging the tables and chairs back into order in preparation for tomorrow. Couples today had been overjoyed at the possibilities she and Nissa offered and had left the café with a hopeful spring in their steps. She'd received a message from Fiona that she and Liam were having a good time and had extended their honeymoon. Nissa was a hard worker and had been like a breath of spring, so when she'd asked if she could leave early to visit a friend, instead of staying to help clean up, Lady Roselyn had agreed.

Lady Roselyn smiled, knowing she had been happy

that Nissa wanted to leave early. She glanced toward William. For the first time in a long time they were alone. She'd forgotten how long they'd known each other. It felt as though he'd been in her life since the beginning. She knew there were things about his past he hadn't shared. It didn't bother her. She had secrets of her own. He'd taken off his tweed jacket, and although he was no longer a young man, his muscles were still toned and his shoulders broad, and when he smiled…

She let out a breath, feeling like a schoolgirl. Chasing away the heated thoughts, she said, "Are you hungry?" She'd blurted out the question before she could talk herself out of their spending more time together.

"I am starving." His grin was boyish as he pushed a chair under a table and walked toward her. "I like what you're wearing, by the way. 'Tis a grand rosy-pink color. I've wanted to say that all day, but we've been so busy. You should wear shorter skirts more often. You have great legs."

She felt her face heat with the compliment. She smoothed her hand over the print blouse and matching skirt that skimmed her knees. "The new clothes were Nissa's idea. I could make us dinner?" She said it as a question. Would he sense she meant it as something more?

He'd crossed the distance between them, his grin widening as he took her hand. "I have a better idea. Come with me, my bonnie lass."

She glanced down at their hands. Every time he'd tried to hold her hand, she'd tried to keep him at a distance and guard her heart. She and her sisters encouraged their couples to take a leap, to move past disappointments and open their hearts to new possibilities. She should take her own advice. Today seemed different.

She made her decision and reached into her pocket for the gift box. "I almost forgot. This is for you. A thank you." She held it out and watched him open the lid, then glance toward her with a questioning expression. She smiled at his confusion. "I know it's a little odd, a solid gold pendant shaped like a fly. It's a replica of a gift Queen Ahhotep of Egypt gave to only her most trusted commanders. I found it in my drawer the other day and thought of you. You could attach it to the set of keys you use for the doors." She took a deep breath. "You are my most trusted friend. I can't imagine my life without you."

He kissed her hand and smiled a thank you. "I treasure your gift. Come with me," he repeated. "I have a surprise for you, as well." He guided her outside and over a path through a canopy of pine trees that led to the creek.

She nodded, loving the way his hand felt in hers: warm and secure.

She hadn't forgotten to lock the door; the truth was that she didn't care. Enchanted by William's spontaneity, she half-skipped, half-walked beside him, feeling years of burden slip away. Was this how it felt when a woman walked beside the person she loved who had promised a surprise? She smiled, knowing that it was never about the surprise: it was that they'd gone to the effort.

"Where are you taking me?" she said, not caring but wanting to hear his voice, that deep baritone that hinted at Scottish roots.

"As I said, 'tis a surprise."

"Have you heard from Duncan lately?"

"Keeping in touch with him with the nine-hour time difference has been rough. I was sound asleep when he called. His message said that the tour was headed for the Etruscan Museum and from there to Tuscany." William kissed the palm of her hand. "If it's all right with you, I'd like to concentrate on something other than matchmaker business—us."

Her pulse quickened. That was more than okay with her. "You are being very mysterious. I've never seen this side of you before."

He winked. "'Tis all about the timing."

William reached the bank of the creek, its waters sparkling in the sunshine and dancing over rocks and logs on its journey to Lake Sammamish. An inviting picnic was spread out on a plaid wool blanket under the shade of a maple tree.

Her heart warmed. She'd created many romantic picnics for her couples over the years. Never had anyone gone to the effort for her. She squeezed William's hand. "This is the best surprise. How did you find the time to do all of this? You were helping me close the café. What gave you the idea?"

He chuckled. "'Twas something Nissa said that started me thinking, and I quote, "What is up with you and Lady Roselyn? You love each other. Be together.""

"Did you tell her our relationship is complicated?"

"I tried."

"And?"

William took her hands in his and turned her to face him. "The more I explained our relationship and why we canna be together as a couple, the less sense it made. Then Nissa announced she'd create a romantic picnic for us today, made me promise I'd invite you, and then muttered that humans were as dumb as moles and walked away."

"Nissa is a gift. Everything is perfect, but did she actually refer to us as humans? Do you think that means…?"

"I dinna want to talk about Nissa." He cupped the side of her face and tilted it toward him "I want to kiss you."

Her heartbeat soared, blocking out everything except the heated expression in William's eyes. She rose up until her lips were a breath from his. "It's about time."

Chapter Eighteen

The tour bus came to an abrupt stop. Genevieve lurched forward, waking from a sound sleep, and hit her forehead on the cushioned seat in front of her. For a split second she thought she'd rolled out of bed, then remembered she was on the Matchmaker Tour in Italy.

The young woman in front of Genevieve spun around in her seat onto her knees and peered over the headrest. "Are you okay?"

Genevieve nodded, rubbing her forehead and taking in the woman's garb—yoga pants and a T-shirt that said *I love Paris* in red sequins. Her name was Cora, and she had been married six months to a computer programmer named Anthony. Bridget had asked everyone to introduce themselves shortly after the bus left the airport terminal and had talked a little about herself being single and having an ability to speak more than four languages.

"The schedule today sounds amazing," Cora said, slipping on a neon yellow baseball cap that Genevieve was certain glowed in the dark.

Genevieve nodded and rubbed the tender spot on her forehead again. "Yes, it does," she said, making small talk. Her least favorite thing.

During the introductions, Bridget had mentioned that in the days to come they would visit more churches, hill villages, medieval towns, and today's highlight, an Etruscan Museum. Bridget also mentioned that a surprise awaited them on their final stop at the village of Civita di Bagnoregio. She also said that although she spoke many languages, Duncan, their bus driver, only spoke Icelandic. The implication was that he wouldn't be much of a talker.

As Cora carried on about how much fun she and her husband planned to have on the tour, Genevieve continued to nod while she bent down to find the journal that had fallen from her lap when the bus stopped.

"I think that's terrible," Cora said, "don't you?"

"Huh?" Genevieve looked up so fast she hit her head on the seat...again. "I'm sorry. What did you say?"

"Our tour guide announced that the couples will take you and Hunter's example and not share a room until Tuscany. Something about distance making the heart grow fonder. My Anthony is pretty steamed." Cora nodded across the aisle toward her husband.

Anthony was helping Daisy lift her suitcase down from the overhead storage shelf. Anthony sure didn't look "steamed" to Genevieve. He was flirting with Daisy. His hair was slicked back off his forehead, and his white shirt was open, showing off a gold chain and medallion.

Genevieve had known Daisy before the trip. She worked as a baker at Emma's Boulangerie in the Village, and until the tour, Genevieve hadn't realized Daisy was seeing anyone. Daisy always reminded Genevieve of the actress Meg Ryan in the movie *Sleepless in Seattle*. Normally, Daisy had a springtime smile for everyone. It seemed she drew the line at someone like Cora's husband. Smart girl. The guy looked like he fancied himself a player.

Just then Jorvy, the man Daisy was dating and who also co-owned the Pisces Fish Market in the Village with his brother, headed toward Daisy. He'd been at the front of the bus talking with the driver and Hunter. Jorvy was usually easygoing. But not today. He moved down the aisle like a fast-moving storm, his gaze focused on Anthony.

"I should go," Cora said, winding an orange scarf around her neck. "I'll meet you at the museum."

Cora must have seen the same thing Genevieve had because she jumped out of her seat and grabbed her purse, casting a glance in her husband's direction. Anthony saw Jorvy's forceful approach and made a dash for the door on the side of the bus seconds before Jorvy reached Daisy.

Genevieve smiled over at Daisy and her knight in shining armor, then bent back down to find her journal, pulled it out from under the seat, and sat back, reaching for her cell phone. She punched in a number and her cell phone hummed to life.

There was a message from her mother, who'd volunteered to look in on Genevieve's cat, Snickers, while she was gone. According to her mother's message, Snickers had expressed her disapproval of Genevieve's trip by managing to open her lingerie drawer and scattering silk panties and bras all over her home.

"No kitty presents for you on this trip," Genevieve said under her breath as she reread an email from the airline saying they still hadn't found her luggage. Hunter's prediction that they never would seemed more likely than ever.

She saved the airline's message and scanned her emails. No messages from Frank. Bridget claimed that distance made the heart grow fonder. It seemed in Frank's case it was more like out of sight, out of mind.

"My life sucks," Genevieve said.

"Are you okay?"

Genevieve jerked at the sound of Bridget's voice and looked around. The bus had emptied, and Bridget stood in the aisle wearing a mother-hen expression. Bridget had transformed from the quiet, matchmaking, middle sister Genevieve had met at the café into everything you expected from a European tour guide. Bridget spoke multiple languages, was friendly to everyone, always in a good mood, and somehow managed to look runway perfect in jeans, boots, and a cloth jacket.

"I'm fine," Genevieve said, and she accepted a guidebook on the Etruscan Museum, tucked her cell phone and journal back into her tote bag, and scrambled out of the bus.

"I was waiting for you," Hunter said.

He'd waited for her. She swallowed down the excitement as she looked up to meet his steady gaze.

He reached into his backpack. "I bought you something in the museum's gift shop. They didn't have bikini tops, but there's everything else from key chains to gladiator swords."

Hunter drew out an oversized, spring-blue silk shawl, with a hand-painted image of the goddess Minerva riding her golden chariot through a Tuscan countryside, reminding Genevieve of a Monet painting.

"The woman at the gift shop said it's large enough

for you to use as a strapless dress, scarf, skirt…not sure how that would work."

She accepted the gift. "It's breathtaking. I've never worn this color before."

He shoved his hands in his pockets. "When I think of you, I think of spring or summer. Not sure why."

She reached up and kissed him on the cheek. "Thank you." The impulse felt so natural.

His hand lingered on the small of her back, keeping her pressed against him. His lips were close to hers. "Everyone's watching us. Should we put on a show?"

His words wrapped around her. She remembered every romance movie she'd ever seen where two friends kissed for the first time in front of a crowd of onlookers. She settled back down to earth and edged away. "I don't think we should kiss. I'm more of a private person, and anyway, I'd mess it up."

"I doubt that."

Chapter Nineteen

They'd escaped the first-kiss scenario. Genevieve should feel relieved. So why did she feel cheated and trembling? Why did every nerve in her body feel on edge? This shouldn't be happening.

As soon as she entered the museum, she left the group. She had to get away from Hunter and clear her head. Things were too intense between them. She needed distance to remind herself this was a business arrangement, nothing more.

Except now she was lost. Just great.

Genevieve had expected a museum with sterile white walls, rooms dedicated to time periods or artists and filled with glass display cases. While the Etruscan Museum shared some of these themes, it also was more creative. Many of the statues were displayed in settings that replicated archeological sites. The effect was dramatic and created an atmosphere in which you imagined you were more of an archeologist making a discovery than a tourist on the sidelines.

She paused beside a marble statue of a young man dressed in ancient Roman garments. She'd learned from her guidebook that in some cases the statues were hollow and served as both a likeness of the person who'd died as well as their tomb. She moved further along the deserted hallway. Statues lounged across elaborate marble boxes or sat in throne-like chairs, as though attending a banquet. The most dramatic was the coffin where a man and woman sat on a bench holding hands. They looked happy and content. Genevieve imagined the couple were lifelong partners who when their time came wanted to be buried together.

The romance of such an outcome tugged at her heart. She blinked away an unexpected tear and vowed it was her expression of joy for the couple who'd found they were soulmates. What would it be like to have a love that lasted forever? She wasn't a cynic that believed such a love didn't exist. She just didn't believe it could happen to her.

Genevieve headed down a corridor of the museum that opened onto a spacious room filled with glass cases protecting gem-encrusted bracelets, dangling gold-beaded earrings, necklaces that were as intricate as lace, as well as rings and priceless statues. One of the most prized in the collection was a pair of gold earrings from the Necropolis, third century according to its label, that had been purported to have been made as an offering to the goddess Athena.

The cases served as a golden frame along the perimeter of the room, as though to highlight the museum's centerpiece. The larger-than-life-size bronze statue of the warrior goddess Minerva dominated the center of the room. Her right arm raised, she held a sword in one hand and the reins of the horses in the other as she rode a golden chariot into battle. The museum's guidebook described an amethyst ring on Minerva's left ring finger. Although the setting was visible, the gemstones were missing, but given the statue's age that was understandable. It had been around for over five thousand years.

Pulled by the statue's beauty, Genevieve drew closer. Minerva's outstretched arm seemed to point down a corridor to the left.

The corridor led to another art chamber. Inset ceiling lights showered beams of light on a series of crypts much like the ones she'd seen earlier. Marble statues of well-dressed Etruscan men and women lounged across the marble and stone caskets. Genevieve was struck again by how lifelike these statues appeared. Not only were their features and expressions full of emotion, but the clothes they wore seemed so real. Genevieve half expected that if a gentle wind entered the room she'd be able to see the silk of their robes ripple in the breeze.

She turned down another corridor, thinking that she'd retrace her steps, only to feel more lost than ever. The statues were all starting to look alike. The air felt cooler, as though she were going down—not a good sign, since the museum's exit was on the ground level.

She spotted a door that she hoped would lead outside, or at least back to someplace familiar. It was made from weathered wood planks, rounded on top, with a latticework of iron bolted to the wood. The only decoration was a raised Scottish thistle burned into the wood.

She reached for the brass doorknob and opened the door. A blast of cold air pushed against her, and mist curled around the opening. She stepped forward, poised on the threshold as another wave of mist hit her.

Dizzy, she shut her eyes for a split second, rubbing her arms against the chill. Once she felt steadier, she opened her eyes.

A cave stretched out before her, its interior stacked

floor to ceiling with wine barrels. A white cat with a black tail, perched on the nearest barrel, let out a shrill meow.

Startled, Genevieve stepped back and into Bridget.

"There you are," Bridget said, yanking Genevieve away from the door. Her smile was tight as a rubber band as she shut the door behind Genevieve. "It should have been locked."

"What was that place?"

Bridget motioned for Genevieve to follow her. "Another exhibit, is all. We must hurry. The bus will be leaving soon."

The museum's alarm sounded. The shrill sound echoed down the corridors.

"Fire?" Genevieve shouted toward Bridget.

Bridget cast Genevieve a wide-eyed glance. "Or theft."

****

The alarm rang in Genevieve's ears as she raced beside Bridget down one corridor and then another, all filled with statues frozen in time. Bridget slowed when she reached the room that housed the statue of Minerva and the display cases of jewelry.

The room was jammed with anxious tourists, and around its perimeter were stationed armed guards, weapons resting across their arms as they scanned the area.

It sent a chill down Genevieve's spine.

Bridget located her tour group and rushed over to them. Genevieve held back, taking her time, watching. Tour groups were easily distinguished by tour directors who spoke to them in their native language. The tourists who were visiting the museum on their own stuck together or joined groups. Everyone was visibly on edge.

At first glance, the room and the display cases looked untouched, but in a museum this size the possibilities were endless.

Genevieve pushed her way through the crowd until she reached Bridget's side. "Do you have any idea what was stolen?"

Bridget shook her head. "No one will tell me anything. I might have to ask…"

Hunter interrupted what she was about to say as he jogged over. "The museum is in meltdown. Someone stole the amethyst stone from the statue of the warrior goddess Minerva."

Genevieve gasped. "Whoever stole the stone could have blended into the crowd or made their escape before the alarm was ever triggered."

"Or left through a door," Bridget said. "Listen, everyone! We will be subjected to a metal detection search before we can leave the museum. Please meet me afterward at the museum's café. I'd planned another stop, but there won't be time. We'll head directly to our hotel in Tuscany. We're all accounted for." Bridget counted again. "No, we're not. Where is Jorvy?"

Daisy rose on her tiptoes to peer over the crowd. "He said he had to make a phone call to his brother back home. Something about a shipment of salmon." Her expression brightened. "Here he comes."

Jorvy jogged over to Daisy and gave her a kiss. "What did I miss?"

Cora shook her head as Bridget rounded up the tour members. "This is a colossal waste of time. We'll miss the olive oil tastings."

Genevieve left the grumbling Cora and whispered to Hunter, "Do you think this is connected to the antiquities theft ring we're investigating?"

"Count on it."

Chapter Twenty

While Genevieve waited for security to release the rest of the tour group, she drifted through the Etruscan Museum's gift store, assaulted on all sides by the selections. Standard key chains and magnet souvenirs were displayed beside more upscale reproductions of Etruscan earrings, pendants, and bracelets, and hand painted silk scarves. Everything with a surface, afghans to Zodiac charts, displayed images Genevieve had seen in the museum.

Avoiding the racks of clothes, she fingered a scarf like the one Hunter had given her. He'd said she reminded him of spring or summer. The memory quickened her heart, and when she looked around for a distraction, a wall of bookshelves caught her attention.

She veered around a group of tourists thumbing through postcards as she headed toward the deserted shelves. Traditional guidebooks on the history of the Etruscans and their art in the museum were offered in over a dozen different languages. Genevieve selected one in English and moved down the aisle. The Etruscans weren't the only civilization featured in the books on display. It was a celebration of Italy, from the Etruscans, Romans, the glory days of Leonardo de Vinci and Michelangelo, to present-day Italy. Books on everything from recipes and customs to religious and political beliefs were for sale.

"Overwhelming, isn't it?"

Startled, she jumped and dropped her book.

Hunter tucked a paper sack with the museum's logo under his arm and bent down to pick Genevieve's book from the floor. "Why the sudden interest in researching Etruscan art?"

He'd asked a good question. Embarrassed, she accepted the book he'd retrieved while averting her gaze. "I'm not prepared. You mentioned this assignment involved art thieves, and I thought I could fake my way through because I know Leonardo de Vinci painted the *Mona Lisa* and Michelangelo sculpted *David.* The truth is we're investigating a possible antiquities theft ring and I know next to nothing about art or its artists, or how to distinguish between a reproduction and the real thing. For example, I know Leonardo and Michelangelo lived in the same century, but did they know each other? And is that even important?"

He lifted an eyebrow as he gathered several books from the shelf. "I'm impressed. Most people don't know that much about those two men, let alone the fact that they lived in the same century. Yes, they did know each other and were fierce rivals. Sometimes they painted the same type of battle scene in competition." He handed her the books he'd collected. "These may help. They can give you an overview of the art in Italy's Golden Age, right up to the time of Beanini, who in many accounts, despite his talent as a sculptor, was a real jerk." He looked over his shoulder. "Bridget is waving us over. Looks like our group is cleared to leave."

****

With her tote bag filled with book purchases, Genevieve headed to the museum's café, where Bridget had asked the group to meet. Daisy intercepted Genevieve, directing her to an empty seat. As Genevieve sat down, a server set down a cup of steaming tea and a brownie with a small candle in it.

Daisy sat beside her and lit the candle. "Happy Birthday."

Genevieve glanced around the table. Everyone seemed focused on her. She turned toward Daisy. "How did you…"

Bridget stood and lifted her hot chocolate in a toast. "As we all know, it's Genevieve's birthday today." She turned toward Genevieve and smiled. "There's a reason we ask everyone to fill out their date of birth. My sisters and I love celebrating birthdays. Normally, if there is a birthday during our tours, we provide a cake, but in light of the airline losing your luggage, everyone wanted to do more." Bridget raised her mug higher. "Happy birthday, Genevieve. Now make a wish and blow out your candle."

Happy Birthday wishes rippled around the table, and when Genevieve's gaze reached Hunter, he raised his coffee and winked before taking a drink. She felt her face burst into flame and turned from him as next Gigi wished her a happy birthday and then Mr. Digby.

"Blow out the candle," the group chanted.

"Make a wish," Daisy said.

Genevieve kept her focus on the candle until the flame blurred. How many times had she wished on a birthday candle? Discounting that her mother would have allowed a one-year-old anywhere near an open flame, even a birthday candle, Genevieve calculated twenty-six times. The wishes had varied from ponies to "Please bring my father home" and lately to writing newspaper articles that mattered. The candle sputtered, dripping wax on the brownie.

Daisy nudged Genevieve and whispered, "Make a wish before the candle burns out."

Genevieve blinked a few times and blew out the candle. The people around the table clapped and cheered, presenting gifts wrapped in elaborate paper of silver or gold foil, pastel flowers, or plain bags with white tissue.

She brushed her damp face with the back of her hand. She couldn't remember the last time she'd had an actual birthday party. Since graduating from college her birthdays were celebrated with her mother, the boyfriend of the hour, or alone. "Thank you." Her voice caught in her throat. "Thank you," she said louder.

Daisy hugged her and handed her a napkin. "You are very welcome."

Chapter Twenty-One

The rolling hills in Tuscany were picture-card perfect. Carpeted with vineyards, bursting with deep, purple fruit and leaves kissed by morning dew, they formed a backdrop to the manor house turned into a bed-and-breakfast. Genevieve surveyed the panoramic view from under the umbrella of centuries-old flowering olive trees. She wished she could enjoy Tuscany's unique beauty, find that elusive center of peace everyone talked about. Even more elusive was the idea that she'd discover her passion. But what was her passion?

She felt like she was chasing windmills like Don Quixote, who searched for chivalry and justice in what he viewed as an unjust world. Passion seemed always over the next hill. So close and yet so far away.

Children were encouraged to find their passion for life in their jobs and in their relationships. There should be a test to know if you'd attained it, or if you were close.

She sighed. She had a job in Seattle that paid the bills, and yet she'd traveled halfway across the world chasing her own version of the Don Quixote story: the quest for a Pulitzer Prize-winning story. Perhaps her mother was right. Genevieve should be satisfied with the type of stories she knew best and concentrate on her specialty. She reported on people losing love and finding love. She was a lost-and-found reporter.

She squared her shoulders and headed toward the room Bridget had assigned.

Hunter swept past her. "Are you anxious to see our room?"

She snapped around and chased after him toward a bungalow on the corner of the compound. "What do you mean 'our room'? We have separate quarters."

"Not anymore." Hunter produced a key and opened the door.

Genevieve crossed the threshold and followed him inside as her mouth opened in awe. After all the mishaps, matchbox-size rooms, rooms that overlooked pubs that didn't close until four in the morning, and railway stations with trains that ran twenty-four hours a day, this room was a dream, and more of a junior suite than a standard hotel room.

The king-size bed had a burgundy comforter, appropriate in wine country. A lavender breeze teased the lace curtains open and had them dancing along the windowsill. In the corner, near a balcony, a large cream sofa, matching wingback chairs, and an antique mahogany coffee table with claw feet completed the elegant feel of the room.

Hunter tossed his backpack onto the bed and laid a bunch of roses on the table beneath the window. "Not as large as the last one, but this will work."

Genevieve rolled the bright pink suitcase Bridget had given her for her birthday over to the bed and removed Hunter's backpack. "What do you mean the room is not large? This is spacious. I could stay here a week. Wait. What kind of rooms did you have?"

"It's not the size of the room that matters, it's the

location."

Genevieve perched her hands on her hips. "Spoken like someone who has always had large rooms on his trip, not someone, like me, whose rooms have been so small the bathroom door bumped against the twin-size bed."

He grabbed a glass from the blue-tiled bathroom and filled it with water. "You mentioned you'd like to stay here a week." Hunter stuffed the flowers in the glass and set them back on the table. "Some people wouldn't mind staying in a place like this their whole lives," he said, looking out the window. He let the lace curtain drop back into place as he crossed the room to retrieve his backpack. "I'll take the sofa."

She eyed the delicate flowers swaying in the gentle breeze. "Darn right you'll take the sofa," she said softly as she opened her suitcase. "How do you do it? You seem at home no matter where we are." She kept her head down. "What's with the flowers?"

He removed his shirt. "The flowers are from under the olive trees out front. Thought you'd like them." He paused. "Home isn't a place, it's a state of being."

His kind gesture caught her off guard. "I love flowers. Thank you. Even the simple kind, and especially carnations because people seem to like them the least. Which makes me feel sad for them somehow." She bit on a corner of her lip. "Sorry, that was a gush of nonsense."

She turned away to avoid staring at his abs and the way his expression had softened when she'd thanked him for the flowers. She cleared her throat. "That whole business about home is where the heart is—that's cool. You're quite the philosopher."

He retrieved his backpack from where she'd set it on the floor and leaned it against the sofa. "It must be this place. It brings out my inner Plato. Plus, I'm better at giving advice than taking it. To be serious, I'm really a survivalist. My dad was a construction engineer who followed the work. Consequently, we moved around a lot. Home wasn't a place, an address where we'd receive mail, it was a home where we were all together."

Genevieve focused on her suitcase, not knowing how to respond. This was the most he'd shared about himself, and she was afraid to break the spell. She fumbled through her suitcase, sorting the packages the tour group had given her to help replace her clothes until the airline found her luggage. She remembered how upset she'd been when she first realized her luggage hadn't arrived. She'd sulked over the new clothes she'd bought for the trip and favorites she might never see again. The emotional attachment to an assortment of shoes and outfits seemed silly now. They were just clothes.

"That must have been hard," she said. "I mean, moving around so much. I grew up in the same house my mother did."

"Advantages to both," Hunter said. "The key is knowing you're loved."

Genevieve pulled out an orange paper sack tied with a pink bow that one of the tour members had given her. She knew without opening it that the gift was from Daisy. She set the package aside on the bed and sat next to it. "This is the first time you've mentioned your family. What are they like?"

"Why the sudden interest?"

She sat up straighter. "Have I really been so self-absorbed?"

"You're entitled. You're struggling with a career change and miss your boyfriend, Fred. When was the last time the two of you talked?"

"Frank. His name's Frank, and I haven't heard from him since we landed in Rome."

Hunter produced a candy bar from his backpack and handed it to Genevieve.

"Dark chocolate." She smiled her thanks. "I thought you only liked milk chocolate?"

He shrugged. "People change."

She stared at the chocolate bar with the logo of the Etruscan Museum sprawled across the length of the black foil wrapper. "Sometimes I think Frank is only with me because he believes my mother will then put him in charge of the newspaper. Or maybe his mood change is the result of him cheating on me. He's showing all the classic signs—he's become distant, late meetings, excuses that don't make sense. Not that it bothers me...which bothers me, if that makes sense. I'm more worried about what other people will think of me when they find out. They'll draw the conclusion that I'm a terrible person and that's the reason he cheated on me."

Hunter joined her on the bed and playfully nudged her shoulder. "You're not a terrible person. You're an amazing person. And your cheating theory is a bunch of cow dung. I don't have any proof on this theory, but I'll wager the excuse you-were-too-busy-to-attend-to-my-needs was used when the first caveman was caught cheating. If someone wants to cheat, they will. Maybe it's the thrill of avoiding getting caught or maybe it's deeper reasons documented in doctors' journals, but the victim is not at fault."

She broke off a corner of the chocolate bar and cast him a sidelong glance. "What about you? Did you ever cheat on a woman?"

He shook his head. "But you can't build a relationship on faithfulness alone. My issue is that if a relationship is too serious I'll end it, leaving broken hearts in my wake. Lately, I developed a two-day rule. I'm never with a woman over forty-eight hours."

"Need I remind you that we've been together on this tour over four days? Although there hasn't been that much quality time together because you're always taking off."

He pointed at her. "See, that's exactly what I'm talking about. If a woman gets too close, she feels she deserves an accounting of my time. The four days we've spent together don't count. We haven't had sex."

Genevieve held the chocolate bar so tight it broke in half. She popped another piece in her mouth. Chocolate usually calmed her. Not this time. She glared at Hunter. "Let me get this straight. You're saying that if we'd had sex, the experience would have been so powerful that you'd have stolen my heart." She stuffed more chocolate into her mouth. "Wow, do you have a high opinion of your lovemaking abilities."

He held up his hands in surrender. "Hold on. Who said it was the woman's heart that was at risk?" He pushed off the bed. "I'm going to take a shower."

"Don't go. I started to ask about your family and then as usual talked about my issues. If we're going to be a team, I think it's best that we get to know each other better. I apologize for jumping to conclusions about your relationships. Truce?"

"Truce."

She settled toward the back of the bed and leaned against the wall. "I've noticed you're a good listener, highly motivated, and independent, which are good qualities for a reporter. I figure you're the eldest child from a large family. You already said that the reason you moved around a lot was that your dad was a construction engineer. So you're flexible and meet people easily. However, because you moved around a lot, you might have commitment issues, which would explain your fear of relationships."

"Excellent, Dr. Freud, and now that you've cracked the Hunter Longfellow code, I'll shower."

She groaned. "I did it again. I made assumptions about you and didn't allow you to talk. Sorry. Why did you let me go on and on like that?"

He chuckled. "You looked like you were having fun analyzing me."

"My boyfriend says it's annoying."

"Your boyfriend's an idiot."

"Please tell me about your family. I promise I won't interrupt."

"But your interruptions are some of your best features. They keep me on my toes, but if you insist, here goes. The Hunter Longfellow story, the short version. You were right about most of it. I'm the eldest, with three sisters and a brother. My sisters are all teachers—well, two are teachers and the third is an elementary school principal—and my brother is a vet. I went against type. Instead of the typical eldest child, being responsible in a traditional job, I'm more of a gypsy. My parents were madly in love and died a few years ago in a plane crash. I think the reason for my commitment issues is that I'm afraid I'll never find what they had. Okay if I take a shower now?" He winked. "You could join me."

The sudden invitation caught her by surprise, and she felt her face warm. The worst part was that she wanted to say yes.

"I…I…" She folded her hands in her lap and counted to five. "What about your two-day rule?"

"I wasn't suggesting we have sex, just shower together."

She narrowed her gaze. "Seriously?"

He laughed, the tone low and primal. A tone that chased through her body from the tips of her toes to the edges of her highlighted hair.

"Yeah," he said, "probably a bad idea. I'll take my shower now…alone."

"We're expected down for dinner in a few minutes."

Hunter pulled his boots and socks off and set them next to the bathroom door. "Bridget apologized and said the cooks weren't available tonight, so we're on our own. She prepared a picnic-style dinner for all the tour members." Hunter lifted the basket with the Matchmaker logo and set it on the table. "I haven't looked, but something in there smells amazing."

Genevieve opened the basket's lid. Hunter wasn't the only one better at giving advice than taking it. He dealt with his commitment issues by traveling all over the globe. She'd convinced herself that, because she'd had boyfriends and had managed a fiancé for a blink in time, she didn't have commitment issues. The truth was that if any man stayed too long, she drove him away.

Because she was never the one to break up the relationship, she kidded herself and the world that she wasn't the one tied in knots with worry about being with one person for the rest of her life.

The shower turned on, and she heard humming.

She investigated the goodies Bridget had provided. There were wine glasses, Bordeaux wine, goat cheese, prosciutto ham, apples, a jar of olives, and a crusty loaf of bread. A feast.

She laid out the picnic on the table in front of the sofa and began to hum herself. A quiet evening with Hunter. Her face warmed again as she opened the bottle of wine and filled the glasses. Then setting them aside, she ventured over to her suitcase and picked out one of the packages, withdrawing a sundress in summer-sky blue that looked like it would flow over her body like silk. She pulled it on and twirled around just as Hunter emerged from the bathroom, drying his hair with a towel and wearing a pair of faded jeans.

His arms dropped to his sides. "Wow."

She wanted to say the same thing about him but kept her focus on his eyes, away from his bare chest and wet hair. She handed him a glass of wine. "You were right. Bridget outdid herself. We have a feast."

"Can't." He shook his head slowly, turning down the wine and reaching for the T-shirt he'd discarded. "Can't. I must…check on something first. Rain check?"

"I could go with you."

He backed toward the door. "Boring stuff. I won't be gone long."

Resisting the urge to throw the wine in his face, she set the glass down on the table instead. She'd thought they were finally getting to know and trust each other, and yet it felt as though they were right back at the beginning. She rolled her shoulders back. "I'll make up the couch for you," she said through gritted teeth.

He hesitated. "Right."

The door shut behind him as Genevieve sank down on a chair by the window and reached for a slice of cheese. She registered that it was creamy and laced with chives. Bridget really had provided a feast. Correction, Bridget had provided a romantic feast, straight out of the matchmaker's handbook, if there was such a thing, and Genevieve suspected there was. She drummed her fingers on the table. She could read a book, finish the wine, eat every crumb of food, and hope that when Hunter did trundle in, he'd be starving.

She stood and snatched up a sweater. Or she could follow him.

Chapter Twenty-Two

This was a stupid idea.

Genevieve buttoned her sweater and headed in search of Hunter. The sun had slipped down over the horizon and surrendered the day to the moon and stars. Had Hunter left the grounds?

She rushed toward the parking lot, but the bus was in its spot and none of the cars were missing. Easy to keep track, as there were only three, the owner's red van and two nondescript silver rental cars so small they looked like they could fit into the van.

She hadn't heard someone drive up, so Hunter must still be on the grounds. Unless he'd jogged into town, her rational self said. Meanwhile, she was freezing to death. It might be spring, but the nights were ice-cold.

"What are you doing here?"

"Looking for you," she said, recognizing Hunter's voice as she turned to face him.

He reached for her arm and guided her behind the trunk of the largest of the olive trees. Its trunk was twisted and gray and reminded Genevieve of the kindly Mr. Digby.

The doors in the main hall opened, and three couples from the tour poured out, laughing. "Get down," Hunter said. "I don't want them to see us. I don't have proof, but I believe the thief at the Etruscan

Museum is connected to the tour somehow."

Genevieve still had difficulty wrapping her head around the possibility the three matchmaker sisters were involved in a theft ring and harbored a sinister side. "If you publish your theory, it will ruin the sisters, even if your claims are later proven false. Why this story?"

"That's why I want to be careful. And to answer your question, Native Americans believe there are consequences if someone steals from the ancestors, and I believe they're right. I'm just doing my part to keep the world in balance. Does that sound too out there?"

She smiled. "It sounds amazing."

He grinned and pulled her farther into the shadows and motioned for her to keep her voice low. "They're headed this way," he whispered. "And no worries, I have no intention of publishing an article without proof. That's why I'm here. But I need a distraction. I've already searched Gigi and Mr. Digby's room, as well as Cora and Anthony's. I tried Bridget's, and the bus driver's, but for some reason I couldn't open their windows or doors. I'll try again at our next location. Could you distract Daisy and Jorvy? I'll need about ten minutes. Fifteen is ideal."

"What do you mean you've searched their rooms? Are you insane? You're talking about a felony."

"Are you going to help me or not?"

She glanced toward the approaching couples. Gigi and Mr. Digby waved goodbye to the others and headed toward their bungalow while Cora, Anthony, Daisy, and Jorvy stayed behind to talk. How was she going to distract Daisy and Jorvy, and should she? She would be helping Hunter break into their rooms, making her an accessory to a crime. Her thoughts spiraled in a million different directions.

Then she swore under her breath. She was as insane as he was. "I'll do it," she ground out almost under her breath.

Without answering, Hunter ducked into the shadows. Cora and Anthony headed toward their rooms and Daisy and Jorvy in the opposite direction. An idea came to Genevieve, and she grabbed a handful of green olives and rushed to intersect paths with Jorvy and Daisy.

She slipped on the wet grass and almost plowed into Daisy. Out of breath, Genevieve forced a smile. "You all look like you were having fun. What did I miss?"

Daisy looped her arm around Jorvy's. "Bridget arranged for karaoke and insisted we all sing along. The biggest surprise was our bus driver. He has a deep voice that had me swooning."

"I have a good voice," Jorvy said with a frown.

Daisy patted Jorvy's hand. "Yes, of course you do, dear. Where's Hunter?"

Genevieve rolled the green olives around in the palm of her hand. She'd forgotten to ask Hunter if she should provide him with an alibi. Which would be better, an alibi, or making him a suspect? This was exactly why they needed to communicate. She glanced at one of the green olives and made her decision.

"Hunter is in the room…asleep."

She popped a green olive in her mouth, bit down on the fruit…and gagged. The guidebooks cautioned against eating olives off a tree. The writer of the article she'd read strongly advised waiting until they were properly prepared by soaking them in a liquid solution of lye or brine. Eating olives off a tree wouldn't kill you, he had gone on to say, but the taste experience was compared to biting into mushy swamp grass. She gagged again, holding her hand over her mouth. The writer of the article had nailed the description.

Daisy put her arm around Genevieve's shoulder. "What are you doing? You can't eat green olives picked from the tree. I think they can make you sick."

The bitter taste spiked through her as she spit out the remains of the olive. She'd known exactly what she was doing. "I could use water or something to wash away the taste."

"There's a tray of chocolate chip cookies and coffee back at the main house," Jorvy said. "Or we could take you to your room?"

She spit out the last bit of olive and grimaced as she shook her head. She was never going to eat an olive again for as long as she lived. "I don't want to bother Hunter. Cookies sound perfect."

****

An hour later, Genevieve opened her room and made a beeline to the king-size bed. She stretched out on the comforter and closed her eyes.

"Where have you been? You look green."

She chuckled under her breath. "That sounds about right. You said you needed a distraction, so I ate an olive that I picked off the tree."

"Those taste disgusting. That doesn't explain why you were gone so long. I started to worry."

She opened her eyes and glanced over toward him. He'd started pacing and sounded worried, which almost made the whole experience worthwhile. She smiled and closed her eyes again.

"I may have over-exaggerated my reaction to Daisy and Jorvy, but I wanted to be convincing. By the way, you owe me big time. I want you to promise me there won't be any more secrets."

Hunter spread the blanket over Genevieve. "You surprised me, Genevieve Grey, and you have a deal. No more secrets."

He sat beside her and brushed the hair from her face. "You've got skills."

She smiled, yawned, and heaved a sigh. "Told you."

Chapter Twenty-Three

The windows in Genevieve and Hunter's room stood open and sun streamed in, all fresh and young and ready for the day to begin. Birds chirped outside, and somewhere in the distance Genevieve heard laughter. She yawned and stretched, feeling more rested than she had in days. She sat up, rubbing sleep from her eyes, and glanced over at Hunter. Dressed and pulling on his boots. He looked yummy.

She flopped back down on the pillow and squeezed her eyes shut. Good grief. Where did that thought come from? She slid her gaze toward him again. "Where are you going?"

"Nowhere without you," Hunter said with a smile. "I was just about to wake you. We have to hurry."

She liked the sound of his comment, *Nowhere without you*. The hurry part she had issue with. She registered that she was still dressed from the night before as she shed her blanket. "I need to change first," she said as she grabbed a yellow print dress from her suitcase. Dresses seemed to be the only kind of clothes people had bought for her. At the first opportunity, she was going to buy a pair of black skinny jeans.

"Why are we up so early?" she said, entering the bathroom and shutting the door. "I thought we had this day on our own."

"Change of plans," he said loud enough for her to

123

hear him through the door. "I'll explain as soon as you finish dressing."

A few minutes later, Genevieve was following Hunter down the gentle grass slope toward the vineyard.

"Bridget said the tour group was invited to help with harvesting the grapes," Hunter said over his shoulder. "The timing is perfect. When I searched the rooms, I made sure I didn't put everything back the way I found it."

Genevieve reached for his arm. "Hold on. Why would you do that? I thought the whole point was not to get caught."

"I want to see people's reactions."

"Reactions? I'd be furious and even scared that someone broke into my room. I'd sound the alarm and ask to change rooms."

"Spoken like an innocent person. Guilty people might have a different approach. Oh, if anyone asks, as far as we know, no one broke into our room."

"Won't that seem odd?"

"I'm counting on it." Hunter reached for her hand. "Let's have some fun. Bridget asked everyone to help with the grape harvest. This will be our chance to gauge reactions."

"Has anyone told you that you are very strange?"

"All the time."

She had a feeling life with Hunter was like existing in the eye of a storm. One step in any direction meant disaster.

She walked beside Hunter in silence as they reached the clearing where the tour group had gathered. What she knew of harvesting grapes, or any type of fruit, for that matter, was limited to the summer in college when she'd offered to pick strawberries so she could do an exposé on the plight of migrant workers. Picking strawberries was back-breaking work. Even harder, however, was getting her article published in the university's newspaper once the farmers found out what she planned. They'd managed to pressure the school into killing the story.

The sun had risen another fraction of an inch. The morning was sleepy and new, and the impulse to crawl back into bed was tempting, but learning how to pick grapes and spending more time with Hunter appealed to her more.

She yawned again when she reached the tour group. Workers were lined amongst the rows of vines and bent to the task of cutting clumps of dew-kissed grapes and placing them in wooden crates. A few men, armed with rifles, patrolled the woods in the event a wild boar became curious. Bridget had said it was for show, as there hadn't been an attack in eons. She'd used that exact word.

Bridget was in the clearing and motioned Genevieve and Hunter over to where she stood with other tour members. Everyone seemed agitated.

"Did you hear?" Daisy said. "Someone broke into all of our rooms."

"Ours too," Cora shouted.

Gigi leaned around Daisy. "It happened to Mr. Digby and me the first night we arrived. Mr. Digby said I'd forgotten where I'd placed my luggage in the room. I told him I knew I'd slid it under the bed, and he insisted I'd left it in the closet." She rolled her eyes. "We had a little tiff over who had the best memory."

"If I could have your attention," Bridget said. "The hotel management and I are appalled at what has occurred and assure everyone that the locks on your rooms are being changed. If anyone would like to change rooms, as well, please let me know. For now, let's try to enjoy ourselves."

As everyone moved to their places to begin harvesting the grapes, Hunter handed her a curved knife that fit into the palm of her hand.

"What's this?"

"They're used to cut the clumps of grapes from the vine. Be careful. The knife is sharp. Keep it with you when we're finished with the harvest. You might need it. Everyone acts innocent, and that's when a guilty person is the most dangerous."

Chapter Twenty-Four

Music played in the background as a breeze drifted through the olive trees. The gentle warmth of the sun that had awakened her this morning matured into bright sunshine. Crates of Chianti grapes were dumped into a wooden barrel large enough for ten people to stand in as the tempo of the music increased and the clapping began.

Hunter had his arms folded over his chest. "This is where young couples stomp the grapes, like in the old *I Love Lucy* TV show."

"I didn't think they did that anymore."

"Me either, but it seems to be a big hit with our tour group. Look over there."

Daisy and Jorvy were helped into the large wooden vat, while others climbed in and started stomping around, holding hands.

Bridget came up from behind Genevieve, laughing. "You and Hunter are next."

Genevieve shook her head, as did Hunter, but she was learning that Bridget didn't understand the word "no." Within a matter of seconds, her shoes and Hunter's were removed and they were being lifted into the vat. The grapes felt warm and slippery under her feet and squeezed beneath her toes. The earthy fragrance of vine-ripened grapes filled the air as she clung to Hunter to keep from slipping.

Hunter grimaced. "Okay, not what I expected."

The tempo of the music and clapping shot up a few more notches as Genevieve and Hunter were pushed around the vat. Then someone picked up a handful of grapes and flung them at the crowd, yelling, "Food fight."

That was all it took. Within a matter of minutes, Genevieve was covered in grape juice.

Hunter leaped over the side of the wooden vat and reached for her hands. She jumped at the chance and let him help her over the side. Together they raced, laughing, toward the nearby creek.

Out of breath, she paused on the bank as Hunter waded into the crystal waters. "Join me. The water is amazing," he called.

She did as he asked, and the unexpected chill sent a shiver through her.

He shed his grape-stained T-shirt. "You're cold," he said.

"It's a good kind of cold."

"I agree." He brushed her grape-stained hair out of her eyes. "You are covered in grape juice."

"I must look hideous."

"You look delicious."

"You look pretty good in purple yourself."

"I wonder…"

She lifted her gaze to meet his. "What do you wonder?"

"I wonder if your mouth tastes as good as it looks."

There was so much she didn't know about him. Always, before she dated anyone, she conducted what amounted to a background check, complete with the schools attended, likes and dislikes, family history, and any past relationships. Frank had looked good on paper.

"You look like you're waging an inner debate," Hunter said. Who's winning?"

"Not sure."

"Not sure you know, or not sure you want to know?"

"Maybe a little of both. Right now, there's something I'd like to find out that is more important. For research purposes."

He moved in closer. "I like research."

She stood on tiptoes and smiled nearly touching his lips with hers. "I was wondering the same about your lips," she said as she pressed her mouth against his.

There was sunshine in the kiss and a warmth that caught her by surprise. He was so full of surprises. She was being playful, but the kiss melted into something more, like robust wine, full of the taste of the countryside and the depths of memories. The kiss deepened. It was a serious kiss that spoke of longing and hope. She wrapped her arms around his neck as he pulled her closer to him, lifting her off the ground.

"I was right," he said. "You have stolen my heart."

The words were around her in a swirl of color and fragrance so powerful they took her breath away. She'd dated Frank for three years, and yet in all that time, not once had his kiss rocked her from the tips of her toes to the depth of her soul. This had to be lust. It couldn't be real. It was the kind of impossible connection that would flame out before a real fire took hold. She had to be careful.

She pulled away, and he must have felt the same conflict as she did as he set her down on solid ground again. The cool creek water swirled around her feet and legs as she clung to Hunter. She didn't want to let go. She had to, but she didn't want to.

"Do you want to go back?" she said.

"Not just yet."

Chapter Twenty-Five

The gentle sun from earlier this morning had continued to grow in intensity and poured down, baking the vineyard. Although flowers turned their faces toward the sky and drank in its warmth, fragile humans sought shelter under umbrellas or trees. She and Hunter hadn't spoken more than a handful of words since they'd kissed. They'd both changed clothes and gone about their business as though nothing had changed. But the electricity between them remained.

Genevieve bent over a vine in the vineyard and picked a handful of grapes that had been left behind from this morning's harvest. It was like finding hidden treasure.

She popped one of the Chianti grapes into her mouth, hearing Hunter join her. "You have to try these, they are amazing."

"There you are," he said. He stuffed his hands in his pockets and looked over his shoulder toward a copse of trees that ran the length of the vineyard. "I'm sorry I dragged you into this. I forgot that you're not used to this life."

She shielded her eyes against the glare of the sun. "You forget. I'm the one who talked you into this assignment."

"About that…"

Twigs snapped in a grove of underbrush a short

distance away.

Hunter turned toward the sound. "Did you hear that?"

Genevieve followed his gaze. The tight groups of olive trees formed an effective wall between this vineyard and the one in the valley below. She'd heard rustling in the underbrush all morning while she was picking grapes. "It's probably just a rabbit, or someone from the nearby village trying to escape the sun," Genevieve said, searching for more grapes.

Hunter headed down the gentle slope to the wall of trees. "That was not a rabbit, unless it's a giant rabbit on steroids. I saw a glimpse of it thrashing around. Stay here. I'm going to investigate."

She hurried to catch up with him. "Slow down. You don't know what it is. It could be a wild animal or a serial killer."

He looked over his shoulder and scrunched his eyebrows together. "Serial killer? Who's the one leaping to conclusions now? But just in case, wait here, or better yet, head back to the hotel."

When she reached his side, she rested her hands on her hips. "I was joking. This is Italy, not the jungles of Africa or dark alleys in a big city. I'm sure it's a local person out for a stroll."

"If it's so safe, why are there men patrolling the woods with rifles like a scene from *The Godfather*?"

"Bridget said something about wild boars, but not to worry."

The branches moved again, and then they heard a low oink.

Genevieve moved around Hunter to get a closer view. "Is that a pig?" She turned back to Hunter.

"There's nothing to worry about, it's just a pig. I've heard they are very intelligent. Some people even keep them as pets."

"Pigs don't have tusks," Hunter said evenly. Hunter pulled her around behind him and took out the small knife he'd used to cut the vines. "It's not a pig, it's one of those wild boars Bridget thinks we don't have to worry about. News flash—I'm plenty worried. They've been known to rip a person apart. What I can't figure out is why there is one this close to the hotel. They usually stay in the mountains."

The wild boar pawed the ground, snorted, and lowered his head.

"Run," Hunter shouted.

****

Hunter would never say he was an expert on animals, but he'd been around enough to know that this one wasn't right in the head. Its eyes were glossy and dilated, and drool streamed from its mouth as though it were either rabid or drugged. The animal was wide-eyed, crazed, and as mad as hell. Giving the animal the benefit of the doubt, he thought it might be injured or frightened to be so far away from familiar territory. In any case, it was poised to attack.

Hunter had told Genevieve to run, and he prayed that for once she'd take his advice. The beast looked about one hundred and fifty to one hundred and seventy-five pounds, with razor-sharp teeth and tusks with the sole purpose of ripping flesh from bone.

Keeping eye contact with the animal, Hunter backed up. There was always the chance the animal would give up. The one thing Hunter knew for certain was not to turn his back. The creature would view that as a sign of weakness.

Hunter eased back a few more steps. This time the boar advanced. Hunter tried to remember the odds of outrunning a boar. He knew crocodiles reached a top land speed of thirty-five miles per hour and the best way to out run one was in a zigzag pattern. Thinking you could out run any animal in the big cat family—panthers, tigers, lions, cougars—was as ridiculous as it sounded. The best advice he'd ever been given in those circumstances was to either carry a gun or stay out of their territory. Surviving a bear attack ranged from making loud noises to making yourself big, whatever the heck that meant, since bears could reach a height of seven to nine feet. Best advice in those circumstances was the same as for confronting a big cat—carry a gun or stay out of their space.

The wild boar pawed the ground and bared its teeth.

Hunter backed up a little more, this time stepping on a dry twig. The sound acted like a call to action, and the animal charged.

Hunter calculated his chances. Stay and fight or run for the hotel? The hotel was too far away, and he didn't like the idea of bringing a wild animal into an area with so many people. Hunter switched the grape-cutting knife to his other hand and pulled his own knife from its sheath in his boot, crouching low, bracing for the attack.

The boar leapt into the air, and a gunshot rang out.

Chapter Twenty-Six

In the safety of her hotel room, Genevieve double-latched the door. The boar attack, on top of everything else, rocked what was left of her normal world. She hesitated for a few moments to settle her nerves. Hunter sat on the edge of the bed, holding a towel to his bleeding head. Together they had killed the boar, but the animal had not gone down without a fight.

Genevieve cleared her throat to get Hunter's attention, motioning him over to the bathroom. He was silent while she dampened a cloth in the sink and dabbed at the crisscross pattern of marks on his forehead. He winced, and reflexively she did the same.

"Sorry. How bad does it hurt?"

"I've had worse." He winced again. "You saved my life. That was quick thinking. Where did you learn to shoot?"

"I saw a man drop his rifle and run when he saw the boar. I acted on instinct. My father was in the military and believed his only child needed to learn how to protect herself. But I only grazed the boar. You're the one who killed it."

She rinsed off the cloth in the sink. He hadn't panicked when he'd seen the wild boar. That had been her first memory when she recalled the events. He'd taken it calmly, as though encounters with wild animals were an everyday thing. "Who are you?" Genevieve dabbed at the cuts on Hunter's forehead.

"Ouch. Not so hard."

"Big baby," she said under her breath.

"I heard that."

"You were meant to. I don't think the cuts will require any stitches, but we should make sure it doesn't get infected. Must be your hard head."

"Ha-ha. My nurse is a comedian." He shrugged around her and splashed water over his face. "I'd better go. I want to make sure our boar didn't bring his friends."

When he started to leave the bathroom, she blocked his exit. "Not so fast. You didn't answer my question. Who are you?"

For a split second his gaze held hers, and she had the strangest feeling that he was about to tell her something. Then he blinked and gave her a crooked smile that could have been charming if it weren't so annoying. She recognized that expression. He'd closed himself off. Again.

He shrugged. "I'm a reporter. Just like you."

"Bull feathers."

His eyebrows rose. "Do bulls even have feathers?"

Genevieve crossed her arms over her chest. "Answer my questions."

"I thought you had only one question?"

She ignored him. "A reporter, huh? Well, tell me this Mr. I'm-only-a-reporter, how is it you know so much about fighting animals with your bare hands?"

"I watch a lot of *Wild Kingdom* on TV."

She'd had enough. She poked him in the chest, pleased when his expression changed from amused to wary. She poked him again for good measure. "Stop evading my questions. You kept a knife with you as though you expected danger. You attacked that animal without a shred of fear. Who does that? Are you an ex-Marine or Navy Seal? Maybe CIA." Her eyes widened. "Oh. Oh! Are you some secret ops person, here on a special undercover assignment? That's it, isn't it?"

It was his turn to cross his arms over his chest. "Nothing that fancy. I told you before, I'm an investigative reporter, and some places in the world are safer than others. I like to be prepared. Has anyone ever told you that you have an overactive imagination?"

She nodded. "Practically everyone I've ever met. But I notice that you still haven't answered my questions."

"Do you need them answered in any order?"

"Has anyone ever told you that you are evasive and annoying?"

He grinned and leaned into her. "Practically everyone I've ever met," he said, repeating her own reply.

She bit back the impulse to smile. She cleared her throat to cover up the fact that she was rather liking the fun of sparring with him. "Are you going to answer any of my questions?"

He eyed her again as though assessing what to say. "I heard at breakfast that wild boars were spotted in the gully below the vineyard. That's the reason I kept the knife on me."

"Okay, that makes sense. But you wielded a knife like some knight in shining armor. That can't be normal."

"With three sisters, I did a lot of running into situations without thinking. Boyfriends that needed to be set straight on the rules of dating my sisters, lessons to be taught if they crossed a line. Stuff like that. My sisters had names for it other than 'knight in shining armor.' The words they used to describe me were 'overprotective' and 'deranged.' "

She smiled, no longer feeling the need to hide her reaction. "I guess I should be thanking you for killing the boar instead of giving you the third degree."

He moved in closer, a broad grin lighting up his eyes. "You're the real hero. I don't know what would have happened if you hadn't shot the animal. You slowed him down, and I just finished what you started." He leaned over her until their noses almost touched. "In the stories, doesn't the knight give the fair damsel a kiss when she saves him?"

She tilted her head. His warm breath caressed her mouth as she nodded slowly, not trusting herself to do more.

Chapter Twenty-Seven

The moment Hunter's mouth touched hers, Genevieve felt as though fireworks had exploded around her. But was it attraction or their shared adventure? She pulled away.

What were they doing? Resting her hand on her beating heart, she drew in a deep breath. "We can't. I mean, we work together."

He blinked as though clearing his thoughts and drew a breath as well. "You're right." He flipped on the ceiling light and a standing lamp in the corner.

The flood of light brought the room into focus. "We can forget we kissed," Genevieve offered. "We are professionals."

"Take that back." He grinned, snagging a pillow off the bed. "I've worked my whole life at running away from responsibility and the whole professional mantle."

Genevieve pulled the comforter down. "You dress like you don't care about what you wear or how you look, and yet you packed a very nice sports jacket. You say you aren't professional and that you avoid responsibility, and yet you are one of the most professional and responsible people I've ever met."

"Smoke and mirrors."

She threw a pillow in his direction. "It is not smoke and mirrors. Why is it that you work so hard to hide who you really are?"

He positioned the pillows against the sofa's armrest and stretched out. "Why do you?"

"You just changed the subject."

"Noticed that, did you? I'll make you a deal. You tell me what you are hiding, and I'll tell you my story."

"Story? But a story is just what I'm talking about. We tell ourselves and others around us a story because it's what we want them to know. But it's not real. It's make-believe."

He folded his arms behind his head and rested on the arm of the sofa. "Not always. Look at Gigi and her Mr. Digby. They discovered a second chance at love and grabbed it with everything they had."

"Okay, maybe for the lucky few, but it's just luck."

"Is it? Or is it that we make our own luck? We must work for it. Maybe, for people like you and me, making up a story is easier than doing the tough stuff. Like admitting that there's something between us."

Genevieve removed a pillow, embroidered with the image of a bird cage, from the bed and set it on the chair. "You know nothing about me."

'I know as much about you as you know about me. You said you read my articles. What we write is the real us. How we view our stories is through the lens of who we are. I'll make a confession, but don't take this the wrong way: take this as a compliment. I knew who you were before we met officially. I follow your column."

She looked over at him. "It's a gossip column about weddings and blind dates and engagement parties."

"You're underestimating its meaning. It's about hope and happily-ever-after stories." He glanced toward the ceiling. "After we met, I read some of them again. They're good."

Genevieve's hands trembled as she folded the coverlet, keeping her head down. He'd won a Pulitzer, and yet he'd told her he liked her articles. "So, what are we going to do now?"

"We're going to pretend we don't like each other and see how that goes."

"I mean about the sleeping arrangements. You slept on the sofa last night. You're too tall. That couldn't have been comfortable. I'll take it tonight."

"How would that look for me if someone finds out I let you sleep on a sofa while I had a comfy bed? They'll revoke my knight-in-shining-armor status."

She laughed. "I won't tell."

"You won't have to. They'll know. It's like how Santa knows if you're naughty or nice."

"We could share the bed and put pillows between us."

He shook his head. "Yeah, I've seen those movies too, and I want to throw my popcorn at the screen every time. It looks romantic, but speaking from a man's point of view—when you're interested in a woman, sharing a bed with her is torture, like medieval stretching arms-and-legs-on-a-rack type of torture."

Genevieve turned away so he wouldn't see her face warm. He'd said he was interested in her. She swallowed. "What are we going to do?"

"I'm sleeping on the sofa. It's the only thing we can do. But you see this as our problem, not something I have to deal with. You are something, Genevieve Grey. Why hasn't someone swept you off your feet and married you by now?"

"Maybe I've been waiting for the man who believes in knight-in-shining-armor badges."

Chapter Twenty-Eight

The next morning at daybreak, the tour bus sped over the highway as though in a race, eating up the countryside like a vintage video game character. Passengers on the bus bounced along, sliding in their seats. A few tried to sleep. Some talked amongst themselves. The rest, like Hunter, were reading. Or at least that was his intent.

What was he doing? He'd accepted this assignment, thinking it was like so many of the others. The guidelines were simple:

Identify the target;

Discover the method used to extract the target;

Apprehend suspect or suspects and return target to owner.

Simple. Straightforward. Uncomplicated.

So when did he lose control?

He also felt further away from discovering a target and suspect than when he'd started. He'd taken on partners before and chosen them for their skill set or, like this one, someone to pose as a wife or girlfriend when needed. In those cases, he made sure he chose a woman with whom he wouldn't become romantically entangled.

With Genevieve, he'd thought he was choosing well. She'd appeared as rigid and unforgiving as Mount Everest. But when she landed in Rome, she'd started to change. He thought the lost luggage fiasco would tip her over and she'd experience a moment of panic. He thought she might jump on the next plane home and he'd have to find a replacement. But she'd adjusted.

Her helping him distract Daisy and Jorvy the night at the vineyard showed ingenuity, and her action at the boar attack showed courage.

Hunter glanced out the window at the blur of rolling green hills and the pink ribbon of sun cresting over the horizon. God help him, he couldn't stop thinking about their kiss at the creek.

Poets spent countless hours crafting words to describe the importance and magic of the first kiss. Hunter had never understood their reasoning. A first kiss could be awkward, tentative, a disaster with too many high expectations.

The kiss he'd shared with Genevieve hadn't felt like a first kiss. It felt deeper, as though they knew each other from another time and place—a time and place where they'd shared a life of happy memories.

He shut his eyes and leaned his head against the back rest. "God help me," he repeated under his breath.

Genevieve peered around her seat and nudged him on the arm. "Can I join you? I have a few questions." With his nod, she slid into the seat beside him.

Genevieve continued to surprise him. He gazed over at her wide-eyed stare. He'd begun to recognize that look. She was curious about everything and everyone. Italy had opened a door for her, and to his continued shock, he fantasized about walking through it with her.

****

Bridget's voice interrupted Genevieve's question to

Hunter as the bus rolled into a parking lot under a canopy of trees. The intercom on the bus came on, and Bridget asked for the group's indulgence while she read from her guidebook.

Her voice seemed tentative, as though reading the words brought them to life. "If you observe Civita from a distance as it clings to the edge of the precipice, the village of Civita di Bagnoregio is like a ghost town, something that could exist only in the mind of a visionary or in a dream remembered. On certain misty mornings, the medieval town seems to float surrounded by a fog of unreality. Civita, like an island in our memory or a figment of our imagination, is connected by a single narrow concrete walkway to reality and to the surrounding countryside; it is inaccessible to modern means of transportation and takes us far away, not so much in distance but in time." She closed the book and looked over the group as though processing what she'd read.

She cast a small smile and continued in a stronger voice. "As the guidebook indicates, Civita is perched on top of a steep hill surrounded by two valleys. Way before the Romans, the Etruscans settled in Civita until a series of earthquakes drove them away. Whenever there's an earthquake, sections of the city closest to the edge drop into the valley. But eventually, people started to return, enchanted by its beauty. For a while everyone lived in peace, but then the earthquakes returned in the fifteenth and sixteenth centuries, and Civita was nicknamed the Dying City."

She paused for dramatic effect, then made the announcement that this was as far as the bus could take the group, but it was safe to leave their belongings on the bus, as they'd only be in Civita for lunch. The offer of gelato to fortify them, as they would have to walk the rest of the way into Civita, was met with a round of applause.

As though on cue, everyone rose from their seats and gathered their coats, purses, and bags. Genevieve stayed where she was, her heart racing. Hunter sat beside her, seemingly in no hurry to leave the bus either.

Daisy and Cora paused beside Genevieve and Hunter's seat. They'd become friends and were inseparable. "Do you want me to save you a place in the gelato line? They might run out of chocolate almond fudge."

Cora's coin-shaped charms clinked together like miniature wind chimes as she hefted her messenger-style purse over her shoulder. "I could ask my Anthony to save us all seats," she offered.

Genevieve shook her head. "Thank you both. No need. We'll be right there." She glanced toward Hunter. "We were just waiting for everyone to leave. There's no rush."

As Cora headed toward the bus's exit, Daisy hiked her tote bag over her shoulder. "No rush?" she joked. "You'll be singing a different tune when the chocolate is gone."

Genevieve laughed. "You have a point. We'll hurry."

But Genevieve stayed until the bus had emptied before turning toward Hunter. "You're meeting someone here." It wasn't a question. She waited, watching the play of emotions spread over his face before settling into his familiar neutral mask.

"How long have you known?" he said.

"That we were meeting someone in Civita? Or that this assignment has multiple layers?"

He glanced out the window beside him. It framed Civita. She'd seen pictures in the guidebooks of the city photographed from all angles and all times of the day and night. None of them had prepared her for the real thing. Mist surrounded the city like a foamy white sea, an island cut off from the rest of the world.

"Did you know before today that Civita was nicknamed the Dying City?" he asked

She nodded, knowing that because his head was turned he might not see her reaction.

"You're right," he continued. "About everything. Except I'm not in the C.I.A. or the F.B.I. I am meeting someone in Civita, however. The plan was to discover who was behind the antiquities ring and turn them and what they've stolen over to my contact." His shoulders slumped. "That's not going to happen."

She sucked in her breath. "And if you don't, you'll lose your job or be demoted and sent to an outpost in the Arctic or Siberia or some jungle." She slid out of her seat and reached for her tote bag in the overhead. "We have to do something. How long do we have? I mean, is your contact already in Civita? If he is…" She paused. "Or maybe it's a she."

"My contact is a he." Hunter stood and put his fingers over her mouth lightly and grinned. "I'm not losing my job, and even if I was assigned to any of those places you mentioned, they're not that bad. And it wouldn't be a demotion. Where do you get such strange ideas?"

She wanted to answer that they were from every

mystery movie and TV show she'd ever seen, and from every novel she'd ever read, but she kept that thought to herself. "You won't lose your job if you can't solve the mystery of who's stealing from the museums?"

"I'll not lose my job, and the world as I know it won't cease to exist." He stepped back. "You look disappointed."

"A little," she admitted. "Now we don't have any motivation."

He chuckled and reached for his backpack. "I have plenty of motivation. I don't like it when bad guys win, and I particularly don't like it when people say bad guys will eventually face karma or their judgment day. A lot of bad stuff can happen until then." He headed toward the bus's exit. "So, chocolate almond fudge?"

She laughed and caught up with him, then kissed him on the cheek

"What's that for?"

She rested her hand on his shoulder. "I like how you think."

Chapter Twenty-Nine

The gelato store stood on the corner. Outside were tables with pink-striped umbrellas. A sign advertised fifty-five flavors, from traditional vanilla, chocolate, or strawberry to coffee, fudge, and brandy-infused confections, to the outside-of-the box flavors of smoky barbeque and garlic pizza.

While Genevieve visited the restroom, Hunter had gone ahead and secured a table. Genevieve spied Hunter and headed past the souvenirs to the table he'd chosen near the checkout counter. Daisy and Cora were over by the display of charms. Daisy held up a charm shaped like an ice cream cone, and Genevieve nodded her approval.

Hunter presented a sugar cone to Genevieve with three scoops of gelato, all different shades of chocolate.

"That's too much," she said, accepting the cone.

"I remember you said once that there is no such thing as too much chocolate. Do you want to sit down?"

She nodded as he pulled out the chair. "Aren't you having any?"

"I thought we could share."

"You are delusional. No sane woman shares her chocolate."

He laughed. "I guess I'd better buy my own."

"Wise man."

As he left, Daisy slid into the seat opposite

Genevieve and spread out her newest purchases. "I bought charms for everyone in my book club. Aren't they adorable?"

Genevieve licked her gelato while examining Daisy's ice-cream-cone-shaped charms. Each one was a different color, reflecting the flavors of chocolate, cherry, and vanilla.

"You're right," Genevieve said, eating more of her gelato. "What gave you the idea?"

Daisy gathered her purchases and wrapped them in tissue. "Cora. She has a charm bracelet and collects charms from everywhere she's traveled. She said she's been collecting for years."

Genevieve took a large bite of her gelato and glanced over at Cora as she was paying for her purchases at the counter. The gold charms on her bracelet glittered over her wrist in the bright store lights.

"That's interesting," Genevieve said absently, taking a bite out of her sugar cone.

Daisy stuffed her own purchases into her shoulder bag and nodded. "She told me she bought a whole bunch at the Etruscan Museum." Daisy stood. "Bridget said we're leaving soon. Meet you outside?"

Genevieve nodded as she finished her cone and wiped her hands on a napkin. She watched Daisy join Cora by the exit, each looking over each other's purchases. Hunter joined Genevieve again, reaching for a napkin. "I bought a coffee-flavored gelato and finished it in about thirty seconds. Do you want another? I'll bet I could be talked into more."

She shook her head slowly as she turned her gaze from Cora and Daisy and leaned closer to Hunter.

"When you searched Cora and Anthony's rooms, did you find any jewelry?"

He shook his head.

"Are you sure?"

"I'm good at what I do."

She gazed over at Cora and Daisy again as they left the store. "Daisy said Cora bought a lot of charms when we visited the Etruscan Museum."

"Cora could have mailed them back to the States, or just put them on her bracelet."

Genevieve nodded again. "Have you ever paid attention to the charms on Cora's bracelet?"

"They're charms."

"What if they're not? You said yourself that the best way to conceal a stolen item was to hide it in plain sight. Cora's charms look like replicas of Roman and Etruscan coins. In fact, most of her charms are shaped like coins."

Genevieve gasped and reached for her tote bag, searching for one of the guide books. She withdrew it and flipped it open until she reached the page featuring Florence and the Medicis. She handed the guidebook to Hunter and pointed to the medal Maria de' Medici wore. "She was buried wearing this medal, but it went missing. Cora has what I thought was a replica that she wears on her bracelet. But what if it's not a replica? What if it's the real thing? Didn't you say that one of the things stolen at the Etruscan Museum was coins?"

Hunter looked over his shoulder and then shut the guidebook, reaching for Genevieve's hands. "We need proof."

She nodded. "We need to get a closer look at Cora's bracelet."

He leaned over and kissed her on the lips.

She pressed her fingers against her mouth and tilted her head. "Why did you kiss me?"

He stood and reached for her hand. "I like how you think."

Chapter Thirty

With the gelato store behind her, Genevieve joined the tour group with Bridget. Bridget's parting advice was to walk as quickly as you could on the walkway toward Civita's Santa Maria gate and not to look down.

Her comment had been met with laughter. The advice to stay on the walkway that ran only about nine hundred feet was obvious. Once you started, there was no veering off. Either side was a sheer drop to a valley that resembled craters of the moon. The second comment had drawn the laughter. If someone warned you not to look down, it was as though they were daring you to do the opposite.

Genevieve rushed to catch up with the group. Hunter had gone on ahead to talk with Anthony and Jorvy. To the casual observer, their conversation looked innocent, three guys talking sports. Genevieve knew differently. Jorvy and Anthony weren't aware they were being interrogated.

Reaching the halfway point along the walkway, Genevieve drank in the view. Bathed in the glow of the afternoon sun, the medieval town of Civita glowed as though it were on fire. If the guidebooks were to be believed, like a flame, the city's allure held hidden dangers.

A breeze rustled through the valley below, sending a flock of birds into the air. Beneath her feet, the walkway sighed in the sway of the wind. She hesitated until the sensation passed, then chided herself for her somber mood as Gigi and Mr. Digby strolled past her.

Daisy glanced toward Genevieve as she caught up with her. "What's wrong?"

"Probably nothing." Genevieve scanned the quiet valley below as though searching for an answer. "I've been reading about all of Civita's earthquakes in the guidebooks and got spooked by a little wind. I guess I am a bit of a glass-half-empty person."

The moment she'd repeated the tired expression, she heard the defense for what she'd said enter her thoughts, reminding her that she believed that thinking about the worst that could happen, instead of looking on the bright side, had been her strategy for everything from shopping and jobs to relationships. *Less chance of being hurt, but also less chance of finding love and happiness*, an annoying little voice in her head responded. She focused on the walkway that led to Civita, putting one foot in front of the other.

Daisy shrugged off her sunflower-yellow sweater and tied the sleeves around her waist. "Well, *you* might consider yourself a glass-half-empty person, but your friends see your generous heart. Most people spout a list of what I call white noise. Their mouths move, and words spill out. It's as though they're experimenting with words, trying them on for size, trying to find the ones that reflect their core beliefs. Right now, I sense a change in you. Italy is good for you. Don't worry. You'll find your words and your happiness."

Genevieve looked straight ahead at the stone archway of Porta Santa Maria, which marked the entrance to the city. They were getting close. Daisy's words had helped. It was good to have friends you could count on.

Daisy paused. "Do you have a minute? I have something to say before we join the group in Civita." She hesitated. "I think Jorvy's cheating on me. I overheard a woman's voice on the other end of the phone when he was supposedly making calls to his brother."

Genevieve felt the weight of Daisy's words. Her friend was hurting. Genevieve had been in her position. Friends and family offered support and tried to say the right thing. It helped, but the gaping hole of pain and betrayal remained. She smiled. "Do you want me to help you push him over the cliff?"

Daisy let out a short laugh and brushed tears from her eyes as her sweater fell to the ground. "You're the best. Thank you for not saying something like Jorvy doesn't deserve me or I'll love again."

Genevieve picked up Daisy's sweater. "Have you considered that Jorvy has a logical answer?"

Daisy accepted the sweater from Genevieve. "Jorvy gave this to me for Valentine's Day."

"It's a hideous color."

Daisy laughed again, and this time the sound was stronger. She gave Genevieve a hug. "You're the best. I'll take your advice and ask him. Wish me luck."

"Always."

Daisy raised her arm and waved to someone up ahead. "There's Jorvy. I'll catch up with you later, okay?"

Genevieve nodded, watching Daisy jog through the Porta Santa Maria archway into the city of Civita with its ivy-covered buildings, their windows filled with hanging baskets of wildflowers, its cobblestone streets and winding staircases that reminded Genevieve of a medieval town frozen in time. Daisy had cleared the gate and was headed toward Jorvy. She hoped, for Daisy's sake, that Jorvy did have a logical reason for all the phone calls.

The air stilled, and another flock of birds rose from the valley below and veered south. The walkway trembled, loose rocks skidding off the sides of the cliffs and disappearing into the void below.

She froze as the walkway rolled beneath her.

"Genevieve! Run!" Hunter ran toward her.

She held out her arms for balance. Should she run back the way she had come? Surely, Hunter didn't mean for her to run into the city. She lived in Seattle, where earthquakes weren't necessarily commonplace but most residents had experienced at least one in their lifetime. The one overriding rule in an earthquake was to avoid standing under a tall building.

Hunter reached her side and grabbed for her hand. "Let's go."

The walkway rolled again, like a wave in a turbulent sea. She dug in her stance and tried to move with the wave. "No. I'm going back. It's not safe in Civita. Old buildings. Crumbling walls."

"There isn't time." Hunter pointed toward the direction she'd come. The walkway was twisting and turning like a rope in a gale-force wind. A midsection cracked and yawned, breaking away and dropping into the valley.

Hunter reached for Genevieve, and together they ran toward the entrance to Civita.

Chapter Thirty-One

With Genevieve beside him, they raced through the archway to Civita and sped toward the center of town. Behind them was chaos. Screams punched the air, and clay pots and bricks smashed to the ground on either side. Genevieve ran silently beside him; the only indication of her fear was the tightening of her jaw and the intense focus of her gaze.

He blamed himself for involving her. True, he couldn't have predicted a frigging earthquake, but he was meeting his contact here with the express purpose of flushing out the thief, which placed Genevieve smack dab in the crosshairs of danger even without any natural disaster.

They swerved around a large section of a stone balcony that had crashed to the ground.

Civita hadn't had an event like this one in years. The townspeople in the city of Bagnoregio, connected to Civita by the walkway, had grown hopeful that Mother Nature had forgotten about the Dying City and moved on to other parts of the world with her earthquakes. Hunter had been told by the man who'd sold him the gelato that many of the shop owners of Bagnoregio had moved back to their beloved Civita, and it had become a place for parties and night life.

Hunter and Genevieve reached their destination. The town's square was surrounded by buildings, with a church at its heart. Bridget and the tour group had gathered on the church's steps, and people he assumed were tourists or inhabitants of Civita were milling around in the square.

Instinctively, he pulled Genevieve beside him. The tremors had subsided, but that was no assurance that another earthquake or the aftershocks wouldn't occur at any time.

"You can let go of me," Genevieve said close to his ear, her warm breath a caress. "I think it's safe."

His pulse quickened as he angled his head closer to hers. "What if I don't want to let you go?"

"You can't hold me like this forever."

"Is that a challenge?"

Out of the corner of his eye he noted that Bridget was headed in his direction, with the tour group following behind her like six ducklings. Reluctantly, he let go of Genevieve, pleased more than he should be that she stayed close to his side. He stuffed his hands in his pockets, resisting the temptation to put his arm around her waist again. When he'd concluded this assignment, he and Genevieve would return to their own separate worlds. They'd never see each other again. The realization crushed against him, forcing him to take shallow breaths.

"You're both safe," Bridget blurted, drawing first Genevieve and then Hunter into a hug. "The tremors have stopped, but the earthquake was so unexpected," she continued, appearing as shaken as the city had been a few minutes ago. She pressed her lips together, glancing in the direction of the townspeople and tourists standing on the church's steps.

Hunter followed her gaze automatically and

noticed a man he recognized but knew only by his first name, Duncan, their bus driver, emerge from the church's entrance and nod slightly at him. Hunter clenched his teeth together, preventing a reaction, and turned his gaze back toward Bridget.

Bridget instructed the tour group to gather in a circle while she explained that lunch would be served in the restaurant a few yards away and that she would fill them in on the sleeping arrangements in case they weren't rescued until the morning.

"Tell Hunter and Genevieve," Anthony shouted, elbowing his way around Cora, Gigi, and Mr. Digby until he faced Bridget. His eyes, dark and cold, narrowed. "Tell them," he repeated.

Bridget gave Hunter and Genevieve a weak smile. "It's not that bad."

"Not that bad?" Daisy said, her voice sounding like the squeak of a mouse cornered by a hungry cat. "We don't have cell or internet service."

Mr. Digby patted Daisy's shoulder. "There, there, dear. I'm sure it's not permanent."

Gigi's smile was warm, and there was a twinkle in her eyes. "John is right. Our cell phones aren't working, but it's the twenty-first century. I'm sure there is a lovely young man or woman working on it right now. Isn't that true, Bridget?"

Daisy peered over Mr. Digby's shoulder. "Where did Jorvy go? Excuse me, everyone. I need to find him."

"I saw him when we first arrived in the plaza," Genevieve said. "I'm sure he's exploring. Would you like me to help you find him?"

Daisy's lips were a thin, white line. But there

wasn't concern in her expression, only anger. "He's probably on the phone."

"We need to get off this rock," Cora said as Daisy left the group. "Why are we standing around talking about cell service? You all can stay here and wait for the next earthquake, but I can't stay here."

All the color had drained from Bridget's face. "We must stay calm."

Murmurs built through the group. Hunter didn't need to be a mind reader to know that when someone said, *Stay calm*, it never boded well.

The only thing to do was deal with it truthfully. "We can't go back," Hunter said, "at least not right away."

Anthony stepped forward. "What are you saying? Who's going to stop me?"

Hunter let the threat roll over him, as well as the impulse to punch the guy in the nose. "Bridget is right. We must remain calm. The reason we can't leave Civita right away is that a large section of the walkway broke away and dropped into the valley. The earthquake could have caused more damage to the walkway's structure, making it unstable. The whole thing could collapse at any minute."

Silence descended like a dark cloud before an angry storm. He knew he sounded unemotional, as though he were describing directions to the Roman Coliseum instead of explaining the possibility that they were trapped in Civita. He stole a glance in the direction Duncan had taken earlier, but the man had disappeared.

Genevieve looped her arm through Hunter's and pulled his hand out of his pocket, lacing her fingers through his.

He glanced down into her smiling eyes. The gesture and her expression did more than warm his heart. Her expression seemed to say that whatever happened, they were in this together.

Chapter Thirty-Two

William walked along the path toward the Matchmaker Café, whistling a Scottish tune. The last few days had been like something out of a dream, and like a dream he had no idea how it would end. He skipped up the steps to the café's entrance and cautioned himself to live in the moment and not think about the past or the future. Overthinking a situation had always gotten him in trouble.

He opened the door, and his smile and words of greeting froze on his lips. Lady Roselyn sat in a chair sobbing. He dropped the flowers and rushed to her side.

"Lass, what is the matter?"

Her face was stained with tears, her eyes red. She held up a news article she'd printed off the Internet. "There's been an earthquake in Civita, Italy. Bridget and the tour are stranded. When was the last time you heard from Duncan?"

"We talked last night. The tour was planning on stopping in Bagnoregio and were preparing to visit Civita. They will have to park the bus and walk the rest of the way over a walkway bridge. Duncan said he was following a lead and thought he recognized someone who looked like Claude, in the town. Duncan thought it an odd coincidence and wanted to check it out."

Lady Roselyn's face turned white, and she twisted the article in her hands. "It's not a coincidence. Nothing that man does is by accident." Her voice shook. "It's all falling apart." William had never seen her this upset, and they'd known each other a long time. The worst had been right after she was rescued from the boating accident. A few years after she and Claude were married, they had gone on what was to be a romantic boat cruise for two. Something happened, and the boat went up in flames. The explosion threw Lady Roselyn clear, but Claude was caught onboard. Only recently had she discovered that he'd survived, and it was only then she confessed her belief he'd tried to kill her.

As distraught as she was then, this was worse. It was as if she weren't surprised that he was in Italy.

William sat beside her and put his arm around her shoulders. "I wish I hadn't told you about Claude, with all that you have to worry about. Forget him. Besides, Duncan is at Civita, and I know him. He won't let anything happen to Bridget or the tour group. He would say if he were here that Claude would have to go through him to get to them, and you've seen Duncan. He's a mountain."

William had hoped his attempt at humor would help, but Lady Roselyn didn't move a muscle.

William pulled her closer. "Let's concentrate on how we can help Bridget and the people on the tour. That's our first priority."

"They are stranded." Her voice sounded hollow. "The only way into the town of Civita is over a walkway, and it has been destroyed by the earthquake." Her head rested against his shoulder as her body sagged against him.

"I'll make some calls," he said.

"It's all falling apart," she repeated.

Chapter Thirty-Three

Genevieve felt hemmed in on all sides. For some reason she, Hunter, and Bridget formed the center, with Cora, Anthony, Gigi, and Mr. Digby surrounding them on all sides, bombarding them with questions or shouting opinions. They each had a plan on how to leave Civita.

When someone suggested they lash together wine barrels and slide down the fourteen-hundred-foot sheer drop down a rock cliff, she decided it was time to slip away. Hunter and Bridget had things under control. Besides, if she heard any crazier ideas, she might strangle someone.

"Stay close," was Hunter's only response.

It was said as a request, not an order, and she liked how protected it made her feel. She squeezed his hand again and made her exit.

The earthquakes and tremors had subsided, birds returned to nest in olive trees, and a few of Civita's cats peeked out from behind blush-pink hydrangea bushes to investigate the city's newest visitors. People she'd seen sheltering on the church's steps during the earthquake had resumed their lives as though nothing had happened.

Shop doors and windows were flung open, the romantic music of Italian tenor Andrea Bocelli floated on the air, and baskets and clay pots overflowed with white freesias and gardenias. The flowers' perfume filled the air as Genevieve inhaled the heady fragrance and strolled past shop windows showing off lace dresses, tablecloths, and handmade pottery in yellows, reds, and blues. There was an old-world feel so different from the commercial souvenir stores she'd seen in Rome and elsewhere.

The guidebooks mentioned visiting Civita was like stepping back in time, and this must have been what they meant. Civita had been a thriving city since the Etruscan era of eighth century BC, moving then to Roman, Goth, and Byzantine control until it became part of the Papal States in 754 AD. Earthquakes had been a part of Civita since before recorded history, and still people stayed. There were times when people were forced to leave, and yet they always returned.

Genevieve bent to smell the fragrance of a delicate rosebud nestled in a windowsill's wood planter. Civita was beloved, and despite the danger, no one would leave her willingly.

She straightened and glanced toward the center of the plaza. The tour group had dispersed, and Hunter was heading over to her. She moved in his direction, meeting him half way.

She shielded her eyes from the afternoon sun. "What was the consensus? Are we going to pole vault over the valley or form a human bridge?"

He laughed. "Heard all of that nonsense, did you?"

"And more."

"Yes, some people had some pretty nutty ideas. Fortunately, common sense ruled the day. We still don't have cell or internet service, but there's activity on the other side of the walkway in Bagnoregio. They know people are stranded, and Bridget believes they'll install some sort of a portable bridge."

"What about a helicopter?"

"Bridget believes that's one of the options considered. We'll have to wait until whoever is in charge makes the decision. Meanwhile, I'm starved. The tour group's already in the restaurant. Are you hungry?" With Genevieve's nod, he motioned for her to follow him toward the opposite side of the plaza.

Genevieve walked beside him, weighing the question she'd been waiting to ask. Except, they were stranded on an island city, facing the possibility of mudslides and more aftershocks and earthquakes, so solving an antiquities theft ring didn't seem that critical, under the circumstances. She chewed on her thumbnail.

"You can ask."

She snapped toward him. "What do you mean?"

He took her hand in his and kissed her thumb. "You took the news of us being stranded here in stride. You also didn't freak out on the walkway. I'm impressed. But you look distracted, as though you want to ask me a question."

"Excuse me, but I did freak out. I froze on the walkway when the earthquake hit, which put you in danger. Remember?"

"Regarding the walkway incident, I prefer to believe that you wanted to give me the opportunity to show off my rescuing-damsels-in-distress skill. Now, ask your question."

She glanced toward him, feeling the warmth in his eyes. He was trying to lighten the danger they faced, not just with the possibility of additional earthquakes, but with exposing a thief. Was he as afraid as she was, or was he better at hiding it? The old expression "fake it till you make it" came to mind, and she nodded.

"Okay. Since we're stranded here, I presume the person you were to meet here didn't make it."

"Actually, he's here. Full disclosure? I think he's always been with us."

"He is? He has been?" She glanced around. "When are we going to meet him?"

"We?"

She pinched him and glared. "Stop teasing. We're in this together. Don't think for a second that you're meeting your contact without me."

Hunter rubbed the place where she'd pinched him. "That will leave a mark."

"Big baby." She folded her arms across her chest and then tapped her foot for added emphasis.

He leaned toward her and kissed her on the tip of her nose. "You are delicious-looking when you're pretending to be annoyed with me. You know very well that I have no intention of excluding you."

"How do you know your contact will be there?"

"Like I said. He's always been with us."

As that registered, she caught sight of Daisy and Jorvy. Jorvy was on one knee, holding up a ring toward Daisy, who gave a shout of joy and leapt into Jorvy's arms.

Hunter smiled. "He pulled it off. He's asking Daisy to marry him."

Chapter Thirty-Four

The tour group moved into the only restaurant open to celebrate Daisy and Jorvy's engagement and wait for the helicopter that would rescue them. The power outage in Civita enhanced the atmosphere of the cozy restaurant. A fireplace gave off a warm glow. Candles, their wax dripping down the sides of empty wine bottles set on the red tablecloths, added to the ambiance.

The tour group was the restaurant's only customers, which increased the intimate mood. A tall man served platters of pasta, but despite the smell of good food, everyone, including Genevieve, was on edge. There was no guarantee another earthquake or tremor wouldn't occur before the helicopter arrived.

Genevieve had searched for Daisy and Jorvy to congratulate them, but understandably they had slipped away. Genevieve was thrilled for the couple. All Jorvy's mysterious phone calls had been to Bridget to plan the surprise. Originally, he'd wanted them to get married at Civita, but the earthquake changed everything.

Bridget also had disappeared.

Genevieve sat across from Cora and Anthony, with Gigi and Mr. Digby to her right. They ate family style, choosing between noodles with marinara and meat sauce, or mushroom-and-spinach-stuffed tortellini.

Baskets filled with breads, bowls of parmesan cheese, saucers of olive oil with aged thick vinegar, and bottles of local red wine took up any available space. Platters of cheese-stuffed ravioli with clams and cream sauce were placed close to Genevieve.

As she served herself, Genevieve thought to check the time on her phone, only to realize she'd dropped it when the earthquake hit while she was on the walkway leading to Civita. Her last conversations with her mother and Frank hadn't ended well. Her mother had seemed pleased at first, when Genevieve offered to take a more active role in running the newspaper. Frank had overheard the conversation and had seemed to agree, then began listing the reasons why it wasn't a good idea. In the end, her mother had seemed to agree with Frank. Genevieve felt as though she'd taken a giant step backward.

She poked at the ravioli on her plate with her fork. Maybe Frank was right. As he'd said, it was one thing to write a column and something else to run a company as large as the *Daily Beat*.

Cora excused herself from the table, saying she needed to find a restroom.

Anthony reached for a serving spoon on the platter of clam pasta, then paused. "It looks so good, but I probably shouldn't have any more. My stomach is bothering me. Cora's too. We probably ate too much."

Genevieve heaped a generous portion of the clam pasta onto her plate and reached for the bowl of grated parmesan cheese. "I hope you both feel better soon."

"Me too." He patted the place on his chest where his medallion usually rested and frowned. "And to make matters worse, I lost my medallion. It must have fallen off when Cora and I were running for our lives. The man who gave it to us is going to kill me." He downed the wine in his glass and scraped the chair against the stone floor as he rose to leave. He reached for the bottle of wine. "I should check on Cora."

Genevieve watched him leave. "That was odd," she said to herself. Hunter suspected Cora and Anthony had stolen the medallion from the Medici gravesite and believed no one would think it authentic so felt comfortable wearing it and claiming it was a replica. But Anthony had just said someone had given him the medallion. It didn't make sense.

"Strange little man," Gigi said.

Genevieve spooned the grated cheese over her pasta. "No argument. Do you know the time?"

Gigi shook her head as Mr. Digby put his hand on her shoulder and nodded toward the door. "Stay and talk a while if you like, but I'm going up to our room for a short nap. I'm feeling a little poorly."

Gigi squeezed his hand. "I'll be right along, John." She smiled toward Genevieve and placed her napkin on the table. "Bridget found accommodations for us in a cute bed and breakfast a few doors away, in the event the helicopter doesn't come right away." She stood, bent to give Genevieve a hug, then joined Mr. Digby at the exit.

Suddenly, Genevieve was alone at the table with enough pasta to feed a dozen tour groups. She speared one of the tortellini with her fork and brought it to her mouth.

"Stop." Hunter stayed her hand. "Something may be wrong with the food."

She rested the fork back on her plate. "The

refrigeration hasn't been out long enough for the food to spoil."

"True, but I recognized the man serving the food. He's the one who followed me on the night I had dinner with Mary and her family."

"You're paranoid. It's been a long day, and we've been through a lot."

"I thought that at first as well. After a traumatic event, the adrenaline rush wears off and people experience a crash, like the dip a person feels after a sugar high from eating bags of Halloween candy. That's not what this is. Our friends' symptoms mimic some type of food poisoning. And I never forget a face."

Genevieve glanced at her pasta. A few minutes ago, her mouth had watered at the thought of eating the delicious meal. She didn't know if it was Hunter's suggestion that the food might be tainted somehow, but now all she could see was cooling clams swimming in a pool of congealing cream. She grimaced and pushed her plate aside. "I've lost my appetite."

He tore off a chunk of bread and handed her the other half. "The bread should be safe."

"You are filled with happy thoughts. If eating is off the agenda, shouldn't we schedule a meeting with your contact? There's something about Anthony and Cora that doesn't fit."

He grabbed a couple more hunks of bread. "Bridget is waiting for us in the church."

Chapter Thirty-Five

Was Bridget Hunter's contact? Genevieve had been looking forward to meeting him or her in a clandestine location, with passwords and hidden rooms behind bookcases. But then, perhaps that only happened in spy novels.

Yet the church wasn't what she'd expected either. The churches they'd seen on the tours were dressed in gold leaf and marble, with stained glass windows and larger-than-life statues. This little church, with its gray walls, stone floors, and plain windows, looked like a poor relative in comparison. Perhaps at one time it had been as fancy as the others but had been stripped bare due to fear its finery would be destroyed in the earthquakes. The effect, however, made the unadorned church feel more reverent than all the others combined.

As her eyes adjusted to the low light, Hunter guided her over to a small alcove of candles and the statue of Mary and the Baby Jesus, where Bridget stood with her back to the rest of the church.

She turned toward them as they approached. "I'm sorry I couldn't bring you in on this sooner. There's much to say and so little time, and right now, we have to concentrate on ensuring that Cory and Anthony don't suspect we're closing in on them."

"I don't think they're involved," Genevieve said, "at least not as much as we first thought. Anthony just said that he lost the medallion during the earthquake and that the person who gave it to him would kill him when he found out it was lost. I know the expression "he'll kill me" is overused and often not meant literally, but I think Anthony was serious. What if Anthony and Cora aren't our thieves but pawns?"

"You believe someone else is pulling the strings?" Bridget said.

Genevieve looked over toward Hunter. "Hunter said he saw someone he recognized in the restaurant."

Hunter nodded. "The guy tried to run me off the road, back in Seattle. At first, I thought it might be connected to past assignments. I've made a few enemies. Now I'm convinced it's all to do with this antiquities theft ring."

"What did the man look like?" Bridget asked.

"Close-cropped hair, face like a ferret, eyes like a predator."

Bridget sucked in her breath. "The man you describe is Claude, Lady Roselyn's husband, which confirms our suspicions. Claude tried to kill my sister, and when that failed, he faked his death. Lady Roselyn found out the truth a short time ago, that he was alive. We're convinced he wants to discredit us and take over the business. What better way than to accuse us of using our tours as a front so we can steal art? Hunter, what do you know about the person who contacted and hired you to investigate this story?"

"We've only corresponded through emails," Hunter said.

Bridget shook her head. "If Claude is involved, it's worse than we thought. We'll have to hurry. The transport helicopter will arrive soon, and I've instructed everyone to go on ahead without us. Hunter and Genevieve, please come with me. It's time you met the Timekeeper."

****

The whirl of helicopter blades roared overhead in the night sky, drowning out Genevieve's questions. "What is a Timekeeper?" And the more urgent, "If we don't take the helicopter, how are we going to leave Civita?"

She started to repeat the questions, but it was no use. There was too much noise, and Bridget was already headed across the plaza toward the restaurant. Genevieve followed, close beside Hunter as they ran to keep pace with Bridget. Beams of light fanned out from the helicopter as it hovered over the plaza before touching down.

Bridget slipped into the restaurant, and the lights from the helicopter cast a miserly glow over the room. Its glow flowed in from the windows in a semicircle of gray light that darkened into inky shadows until it turned pitch black.

Bridget flipped on a flashlight. "Stay close. I'm not sure what we'll find."

Hunter reached for Genevieve's hand as they followed Bridget's beam of light through the restaurant and into the kitchen. She paused at a door, her hand poised over the handle. "This was a bad idea. I shouldn't have involved you two. If you hurry, there's still time to make the transport."

"You said it yourself—you don't know what to expect," Genevieve said. "We're not leaving you alone. Strength in numbers, right, Hunter?"

He placed a kiss on her forehead and she felt the

smile in his touch. "You are fierce, Genevieve Grey."

Bridget heaved a sigh as she turned the handle. "Thank you both. I knew I was right about you two. I hope no one is afraid of spiders. I don't think we have to worry about rats because of all the cats in Civita. But be careful. The ceilings are low and the stairs uneven. The tunnels we're about to enter are thousands of years old, and no one knows for certain who the original builders were, let alone the purpose. Originally, the tunnels led to the town of Bagnoregio, where we had our gelato, and they may have been used to transport goods and store food, as the tunnels stay cool year round. We suspect the early Christians may have used them to escape persecution, and later the pagans to escape torture and the prospect of being burned as witches. The tunnels were also used to bury their dead. The most common use these days is as wine cellars." Bridget opened the door and motioned for them to follow her. "I apologize. I slipped into tour director mode again. Occupational hazard, I'm afraid. Stay close. The tunnels are confusing."

Genevieve kept her shoulders hunched down, as did Hunter, as they descended the stairs, following Bridget down a tunnel. Bridget was the only one who could walk without bending over.

With only the glow of the flashlight to guide them, Bridget led the way down one narrow tunnel and then another. They heard the constant drip of water, the scurry of animals, and the occasional meow.

A tremor shook a handful of dust off the ceiling. Bridget paused, and the flashlight shook slightly. When the dust settled, she continued, entering a circular chamber lit with torches. A man Genevieve recognized as Duncan, their bus driver, stood with his arms folded across his broad chest.

Duncan's gaze lingered on Bridget before shifting toward Genevieve and Hunter. "Did they confirm our suspicions?"

Bridget nodded. "They identified Claude."

"This could have been avoided if your sister had allowed me to take care of him in the first place."

"She wanted to give him a second chance."

"Lady Roselyn's kind heart will get one of us killed someday. "I spotted Claude heading toward the underground tunnels. His special skill set is explosives, and I think he plans on setting off an explosion that will destroy what is left of the city. When the dust settles and teams are sent in to sift through the bodies and debris, it will look like another earthquake set off a chain reaction in the boiler rooms and heating systems. It will be declared an accident."

"That's insane. We're all stranded here," Genevieve said. "If he blows up Civita, he'll die along with everyone else."

Duncan exchanged a glance with Bridget. "Maybe not."

Another tremor rolled over the ground, this one lasting longer than the first. A mixture of dirt and pebbles showered down from the ceiling.

Genevieve shook dirt from her clothes. "That can't be good."

"If you need my help disarming the bomb, I've had a little experience," said Hunter.

Duncan stepped aside, exposing a wooden box. "No need. I was able to freeze the countdown mechanism, but it won't hold long. We have to bring it to our thief."

"What you're talking about is impossible unless you have special equipment."

Duncan reached for the pocket watch in his vest. "This is all I need." He turned toward Bridget. "Didn't you at least tell them who I am and what I do?"

"You are not easy to explain."

"I disagree. I'm a Timekeeper. Although I feel more like a time fixer than a keeper. My job is to go into a time period the sisters have visited and make sure no one has done or said anything that might alter history. We knew something was wrong when the doors that transport the sisters' guests back in time were malfunctioning." Duncan glanced at his watch. "We should be going. Our thief won't stay put for long. Plus there's always the chance that the earthquake that's coming will spill into the area in Italy where we're headed."

Duncan and Bridget headed toward a tunnel as though this was the sort of thing discussed every day.

"Was Duncan talking about time travel?" Genevieve said.

Chapter Thirty-Six

Keeping close, Genevieve followed Hunter, Bridget, and Duncan down a tunnel that looked older than the rest. Casket-size alcoves were stacked on top of each other on either side of the passageway, and although they were empty, cold air with the smell of death and decay swirled around them, reminding Genevieve of their use as burial chambers.

The tunnel opened into a room with a pyramid of wine barrels displayed in the center and a lone door at the far end encased with iron latticework that crisscrossed its wood panels. Several cats—one calico, another a tabby, and one with white fur and a black tail—peered out from behind a wine barrel. The one with the black tail leapt onto the top of the barrel pyramid and settled there, licking its paw. Genevieve resisted the impulse to pet the white cat. Feral cats behaved more like their tiger cousins than their domesticated brothers and sisters.

Genevieve smoothed her hand over the seasoned wood that was as dark as the iron that held it in place. "I've seen a door like this one before, and this place looks familiar, as well. I was in the Etruscan Museum and was lost. I opened a door, hoping to find an exit. What caught my attention there was the cat with the black tail. It reminded me of the one in the retail Village close to where I work. Bridget stopped me from entering, saying it was a new exhibit and still under construction."

"I couldn't tell you the truth," Bridget confessed. "That has all changed. What we're about to do is something many novelists and scientists, including the great physicist, Dr. Stephen Hawking, have debated. I'm talking about time travel. Many credit H. G. Wells, who wrote *The Time Machine* in 1895, as the first to conceptualize the use of a vessel or vehicle for time travel. The author Enrique Gaspar y Rimbau wrote a time travel story in 1887. In fact, time travel was a common theme in Celtic, Hindu, Buddhist, Japanese, Native American, and Jewish mythology, to name a few. The matchmaker's device is a combination of both science and magic, but I don't know how it really works. Those secrets are tightly held by our council. What I know is that a year is placed on a door that corresponds to a door in another time. Once the door is activated, it operates like H. G. Wells' time machine. The doors are activated at midnight."

"It's past midnight," Genevieve said.

"Every rule," Bridget said, "has its exception. The ancients who created time travel knew safeguards were needed to protect time from corruption. Timekeepers like Duncan are those safeguards. They can travel anytime they want." She glanced toward Duncan. "Is it time?" With his nod, she continued, "I must warn you that the first time you walk through to the other side the experience can be disorienting. The farther back in time a person travels, the more dramatic the experience. Some people throw up, some fall asleep, others can't stop giggling. The experience varies. However, it shouldn't be that bad, as we won't be traveling back in time, just to another location hundreds of miles away, but I wanted to warn you. Any questions? No? Shall we go, then?"

****

Before Genevieve could respond, the door opened, and an ice-cold mist smothered Genevieve. She couldn't breathe. She shut her eyes and gasped for air. Nudged from behind, she stepped forward, and in the next instant warm air replaced cold.

She opened her eyes and stumbled forward into the hallway of the Etruscan Museum. She gasped and stifled the impulse to scream. Bridget had explained what would happen, and Duncan had given them their assignments, but how was it possible? Hunter and Bridget were already there, and she rushed forward as Duncan materialized behind her. No time to think...or panic. She had her assignment. Duncan gave a clipped nod, and they all took off to their prearranged areas, Hunter to the north, Duncan the west, Bridget the east, and Genevieve the south.

According to Duncan, they had to find Claude and stop him before he left the museum. If he made it to Rome, he'd have countless doors available that he could use to transport him back in time to any place in history. Bridget's admission that she didn't know how time travel worked reminded Genevieve of her own understanding about the combustion engine in her car. She knew if the ignition turned on she was in business, but she hadn't a clue how the engine worked.

She'd chosen the section that had one of the museum gift shops near the display of the museum's collection of priceless Etruscan jewelry.

There had been a failed attempt to steal one of their

most prized pieces: the earrings of the goddess Athena. They were a chandelier-style, solid gold, four or five inches in length, with a gold image of the goddess. Five chains dangled from each arm and at the ends were solid gold doves.

When Genevieve rounded the corner, she recognized the man from the restaurant in Civita as he ducked into the gift shop to hide from view. He must be Claude. He had smashed the glass case and was stuffing bracelets, necklaces, and earrings into a messenger-style bag. An alarm should have gone off by now. He must have found a way to disarm it, and from the look of the case, he was almost finished stealing all the jewelry.

She had to stop him, stall for time. If she made enough noise, maybe someone would hear her. She crept away from the display counter and shouted, "The police are on their way!"

The man's shoulders stiffened, and when he turned, his face looked like the mask of a vengeful god. "I doubt that seriously. The sisters wouldn't risk exposing their secret."

His sneer dismissed her words, and turning his back to her, he smashed the last display case with a stone head artifact. Glass shattered and showered to the floor.

She needed a weapon.

The gift shop in the museum specialized in replicas of the Etruscan artifacts, and she remembered a case filled with life-size, Roman-style swords. She raced toward the back of the shop. The case was right where she remembered, and it looked like Claude had already smashed the lock. She reached in, grabbed a sword, and then raced back toward Claude.

Genevieve held the sword out in front of her toward Claude. "Thief, I told you to stop what you're doing!"

He turned his head toward her as though about to swat away an angry insect, and then his eyes widened. "I'm impressed, but you have no idea how to use one of those, do you?"

She widened her stance. "I'm a fan of *Lord of the Rings* and historical movies. I understand the basics. I use the pointy end to stab the bad guy. FYI, you're the bad guy."

"This is not your fight. This is between me and the matchmakers. I'll leave them alone to match as many delusional souls as they like. All I want is the opportunity to live the life I deserve. Taking a few artifacts and selling them is a small price for my silence."

Suddenly Hunter was there, rushing in from the opposite side of the room. "You steal art that doesn't belong to you. That makes it our business."

"I sell it back to museums or private collectors. You make it sound as though I destroy the things I take."

"You make it sound as though no one gets hurt," Genevieve said.

"So what?"

Hunter moved closer to him. "There is a legend my people tell that when you steal from its resting place an object made by an ancestor, negative energy escapes. This energy can seep into the thief and blacken his soul, or it can change the atmosphere where the object was stolen. You need to return those artifacts before more people are hurt."

Claude clutched the messenger bag against his chest. "It's all mine."

Genevieve turned toward Hunter. "Is it just me, or does Claude sound like Gollum in *Lord of the Rings*? If he calls it his precious, I'll…"

Claude pulled a gun from his belt and trained it on Genevieve, motioning for her to drop her sword. "Where's the Timekeeper?" Claude shouted.

Bridget emerged from around the corner of another hallway. "He's on his way."

Claude stepped over to Bridget, grabbed her arm and held the gun wedged against her side with his other hand. "Where is the Timekeeper?" he repeated.

"You should release Bridget," Duncan said, coming into view from his direction.

Claude whirled at the sound of Duncan's voice. Then his gaze zeroed in on the bomb Duncan held. "It's ticking."

"You're not as dumb as you look."

"You aren't going to blow us all up," Claude said.

"And you don't know much about the Timekeeper's code, do you? Death before discovery. Hand your weapon over to Hunter, and I'll disarm the bomb."

Chapter Thirty-Seven

The moment Claude handed his weapon over to Hunter, the ticking stopped. Duncan secured Claude's hands in a zip-tie as Bridget left to contact her sisters and tell them Claude had been captured.

"How are Anthony and Cora involved?" Genevieve said.

Claude laughed, the noise like the rattle of chains. "Your fiancé said you were clever, so I used them to take the heat off me. Here is a multiple-choice question for you. Choose one—A. I planned this on my own. B. I have a cadre of minions who will track you all down and make you pay. C. It's all about the money. Or D. I'm only the puppet, not the puppeteer."

Genevieve's heart seemed to stop. Why had Claude mentioned Frank? She took in slow, even breaths. The immediate danger was Claude and the hate that poured from him. She was certain he'd left out the part about revenge, but there was a little truth in all the answers, except the part about him doing this on his own. What he'd been able to accomplish was something bigger than one person.

"We'll find out the truth," Hunter said. "Secrets don't stay hidden forever, no matter how deeply they are buried."

"You're not as smart as you think," Duncan said, nodding toward Claude. "We caught you. Tell us where you've hidden the art you've stolen. Hunter's theory that the doors malfunctioned because objects were stolen from one time and brought into another is correct. That's why Timekeepers were established. I can restore order if you turn over what you've stolen."

"You must think me the fool. Once I tell you their location, I'll have turned over the means that will make me a wealthy man and rendered myself expendable. I'll take my chances, since I'm the one who will choose my prison. I'm thinking marooned on the island of Elba with Napoleon after his defeat at the Battle of Waterloo would suit me. I'll make the case that listening to Napoleon whine about his betrayal would be torture."

Duncan shook his head and held Claude's arm in a vise-like grip. "Think again. My orders were that if you weren't cooperating, I could choose your prison. We're in Italy, and I've selected a dungeon at the height of the witch trials in the fifteenth century as the perfect place for you."

Claude pulled against Duncan's hold on him, to no avail. "You can't do that. I'm descended from one of the original matchmaker families. In the case of a transgression, I have the right to choose my own prison."

"Normally, that would be true, but you tried to kill one of the matchmaker sisters. That changed the rules."

Chapter Thirty-Eight

A few hours later, Hunter held a first-class ticket back to Seattle, compliments of the matchmaker sisters, as he sat beside Genevieve in the da Vinci airport terminal, pretending to read a newspaper. He couldn't concentrate. Genevieve had received a first-class ticket as well, and they were all checked in.

Instead of taking advantage of the first-class lounge at the airport, they'd decided to wait for their plane in the terminal. The never-ending stream of people, the hum of conversation, and the plane arrival and departure announcements gave a sense of normalcy in an otherwise confusing experience.

It had all seemed surreal. Time travel. He couldn't wrap his head around what had happened. Maybe he wouldn't ever understand.

"Claude mentioned my fiancé thought I was clever," Genevieve said, breaking into his train of thought. "How would he have known about Frank?"

"Didn't you mention Frank insisted you take this tour?"

"True, but I'm the one who brought it up, as well as your involvement. Maybe I'm overthinking things. Claude may have wanted to know all he could about the people taking the tour. Frank was in the Village almost every day. Claude may have noticed Frank and me together and struck up a casual conversation to gain information about me."

Hunter folded his newspaper and set it aside. "True. There is another explanation, but this is a tough question." He reached over and took her hand in his, meeting her gaze. "Do you know of any reason why Frank would want you dead?"

Genevieve rested her head on his shoulder. "None of this makes any sense. It's true that my mother was reluctant to sell the *Daily Beat*, but with her only child dead, and overwhelmed with grief, there's a high possibility Frank could talk her into selling. He was pushing us in that direction. The only thing I can't figure out is that because Frank and I aren't married, what would he gain from my death?"

Hunter put his arm around her shoulder and glanced toward a line that formed at the airline's check-in desk. He'd experienced betrayals over the course of his lifetime, and they never got easier to digest, even when you saw them coming. His had run the gambit from fellow writers trying to steal his stories to threats on his life.

Genevieve turned toward Hunter. Her face was streaked with tears, her hands clenched in fists in her lap. "He's going to get away, isn't he? With Claude taken into custody by this mysterious matchmaker council and taken to who-knows-where, it's our word against Frank's."

"Your mother would believe you," Hunter pointed out, "but you're right, you can't use the reasoning that Frank forced you on the tour."

Frank hadn't physically shoved her onto the plane to Italy. She'd made the decision on her own. At first, Hunter had been upset that Duncan had taken Claude into custody instead of turning him over to the local authorities. But Claude's claims of a secret matchmaker society that had been around for centuries and could travel back in time by opening a door most likely would have granted him a ticket to a psych ward, and the possibility of release rather than a jail cell. If Genevieve's fiancé spun the same story, no doubt he'd receive the same treatment. If only there was a way they could force Frank to confess…

"It's almost time for our plane to board," Genevieve said in a flat voice as she stood. "I'm going to buy a book. Something nonfiction, about a topic that will take my mind off Frank. I've always wanted to learn how to quilt. People who quilt seem so happy, and my mother said it was a skill she'd always wanted to learn, but she was always so busy and never had the time. Did I ever tell you she was an investigative reporter? You called me fierce, but people often compared my mother to one of the first war correspondents, Martha Gellhorn, the woman who married Hemingway. My mother and father met while she was reporting on the conflict leading up to the Gulf War in the late 1980s and early nineties. My father was stationed in the Middle East at the time and said she was as cool under fire as any soldier he'd ever met."

She rubbed her hand over her face. "Sorry. I'm so tired I'm rambling. I'm going to find a payphone and call my mother and let her know when we'll arrive."

Genevieve started to head over to the airport's variety store which sold everything from magazines, souvenirs, books and food, but Hunter stood as well.

"I never knew that about your mother, but you've given me an idea. When you call your mother, make sure you tell her not to let Frank know we're alive."

Her eyes widened. "Excuse me?"

"This is going to sound wild, and the plan in my head is in its beginning stages, but if it works, we might have a chance of exposing Frank for the bottom feeder he is."

"That's a big 'if,' but what do you have in mind?"

Chapter Thirty-Nine

William's limo parked at the curb of the villa on the outskirts of Rome. The day was blistering hot and the sun blinding. He never understood why people chose to vacation here, let alone live here permanently. He preferred the cool breezes over the Highlands of Scotland, where you could walk outside in the afternoon without feeling like you'd entered an oven. The only reason he was here was that he'd received an urgent message from Duncan, saying that the situation with Claude was worse than they'd thought.

William remembered Lady Roselyn's reaction when she heard Claude was in the same area as Bridget and her tour. She'd said it was all falling apart. At the time, he'd believed she meant the earthquake and had been worried about her sister's safety. After talking to Duncan, he wasn't so sure.

William couldn't use an enchanted door to travel to Rome. It was too risky until Duncan and his fellow Timekeepers sorted out the issues. The only option left for William was to fly his private jet.

Duncan had transported Claude from the Etruscan Museum to a secure location before the Italian authorities arrived. The next step would be to transfer Claude to the council's guards, who would take him in for questioning and then judgment.

First William had a few questions of his own. He

hated that he hadn't told Lady Roselyn that Claude had implicated the sisters. Claude's claim was outrageous and dangerous. The doors weren't working properly, and they were William's responsibility. When William had learned that Hunter Longfellow was investigating art thefts that coincided with matchmaker adventures, William thought it was a farfetched theory. Nevertheless, he'd hired Hunter to investigate. Never leave a stone unturned was his motto. After his conversation with Duncan, William wished he had left this problematic stone alone.

William left the air-conditioned limo, braced for the inferno, and climbed the steps to the villa. The carved double doors opened the moment he reached the top step.

"Claude's in a secure room," Duncan said. "He's not going anywhere. Do you want to interrogate him by yourself?"

"'Tis best if I do it. What is the status of the door I mentioned?"

"Fully operational."

William nodded. "Lead the way."

Claude was seated in a windowless room. The man wore black tailored pants and a crisp white shirt. Claude liked his luxuries. Duncan had mentioned Claude wanted a deal in exchange for his silence. When the door closed, leaving them alone, William pulled up a chair opposite Claude and got straight to the point.

"You are accused of stealing art from the past, then smuggling it and selling it in the present. This is a violation, punishable by banishment or worse. In addition, you planned to cover your tracks with murder. What do you have to say in your defense?"

"All true. I'll tell you everything you want to know, including where I've hidden the art, but I'll want something in return."

William eyed Claude. The man was calm, confident, as though he was the one conducting the interrogation, not William. "Let's start with why you stole art from the past. You must have suspected that could cause a ripple effect that would disrupt the enchantment of the doors," William said.

Claude shrugged. "That whole time-travel, space-time-continuum, cause-and-effect mumbo-jumbo was never my thing, and anyway, I never made the connection. I wanted the money and to be rich beyond my wildest dreams, and I have pretty big dreams." Claude fingered a gold charm that hung from a chain around his neck. "In the past, security in museums and the homes of nobles was almost nonexistent. All that gold and treasure lying around, begging to be stolen. Why should the matchmaker sisters get to keep all that treasure? There's enough to go around."

William leaned toward Claude. "What treasure?" he said evenly. "The matchmaker sisters operate at a loss. Their inheritance is what keeps them operational."

"Is that what they call it? Their inheritance? That's rich—pun intended. They have doors that open onto wealth that would make the gold discovered in the cave of Ali Baba and the forty thieves look like pocket change. One of the sisters' cousins told me her secret before she gave me this charm as proof of how easy it was to steal treasure from the past with no one the wiser." Claude held it out toward William for inspection. "Do you recognize the design? It's quite unique. It and others like it were stolen from the

Egyptian Museum in Cairo."

The solid gold pendant was in the shape of a stylized fly. He did recognize the charm. It was identical to the one Lady Roselyn had given him. "It's a replica. Queen Ahhotep awarded these golden flies to her commanders for their military service."

"You know your history. However, this is not a replica. It's the real thing, and from the stunned look on your face, you know I'm right, as you've seen one like it before. Perhaps worn by one of the sisters."

William met Claude's gaze. "What are you implying?"

Claude smirked. "You know exactly what I'm implying. The matchmaker sisters' operation cloaks a dark secret. They are a clan of grave robbers. That's how they've been able to accumulate a vast fortune while their business operates at a loss. They don't get their hands dirty digging up graves: they merely open a door to the treasure room in a king's or queen's castle—or in the case of this trinket that belonged to Queen Ahhotep, in a museum in Cairo."

"You're lying."

"Am I? Everyone believes that I tried to kill Lady Roselyn. Perhaps it was the lady who tried to kill me. With me dead, Lady Roselyn and her sisters' dark secret remains a secret."

William's heart sank. When Duncan had first told him Claude was accusing the sisters of stealing from the past, William hadn't believed it was true. Claude's ludicrous accusation was a desperate attempt to secure a deal for his silence.

That still could be the case. Unfortunately, Claude had created a story that some on the council might believe. Especially if this mysterious cousin were real. Even if the sisters were proven innocent and exonerated of wrongdoing, doubt would have been planted and the future of their using the doors placed in jeopardy. William wouldn't allow that to happen.

He kept the anger from his voice. The next step hinged on Claude trusting that William was on his side.

"You mentioned a deal. What do you want for your silence?"

Claude sat back in his chair. "Finally. A man who understands. I want to disappear and live like a king, a noble, or one of those lairds of Scotland. I'd look good in a kilt, don't you think? It makes no difference to me where, as long as I have more money than Midas. I'll let you work out the details."

Chapter Forty

Dorothy Grey's office at the *Daily Beat* reflected the part its owner was about to play. An international newspaper was spread open in the center of her desk and the article on the earthquake in Civita, Italy circled. For this occasion, Dorothy wore a gray suit and a somber expression.

"You look ready," Lady Roselyn said. Dorothy looked up from the article that Lady Roselyn estimated Dorothy had read at least a half-dozen times or more. She couldn't imagine the torment Dorothy had experienced when she'd learned what had happened. Her daughter had almost been killed.

"How could I have been so wrong about Frank?" Dorothy said.

Lady Roselyn was seated in one of the two chairs positioned on the other side of Dorothy's desk. "You're asking the wrong person. Claude fooled me, as well. He told me all the things I wanted to hear." She fingered the cameo brooch attached to her collar, the brooch he'd given her the day he'd begged for forgiveness and a second chance. She'd worn it today to remind her of what was at stake. When their business with Frank was concluded, she was determined to find out where the brooch had come from and return it to its owner. She let her hand drop to her lap. "I wanted to believe people could change. I still do, but Claude is not one of them."

She paused. "I know that now."

"Do you think Hunter and Genevieve's plan will work?" Dorothy said.

There was a knock on the door.

"Come in," Dorothy's voice held a slight tremor.

Frank waltzed in, a smile spread wide across his face as though he planned to pose for a portrait. His expression froze in place when he noticed Lady Roselyn. He recovered, shifting the flowers he held to his left hand and held out his right. "I don't know if we've met formally. You are one of the owners of the Matchmaker Café, correct?" He shifted his gaze toward Dorothy. "I wasn't aware you had a meeting scheduled. I can come back later."

Dorothy shook her head. "Don't be silly. Of course you can stay."

"These are for you." His chest puffed out as he held out the bouquet of orange carnations, wrapped in grocery store plastic. The flowers drooped and looked starved for water, as though he'd purchased them the night before. He removed the purple tulips from the vase near Dorothy's windowsill and replaced them with the carnations. "Have you heard from Genevieve? I told her I'd pick her up at the airport when she arrived." He crumpled the paper wrapping into a ball and arched it toward the receptacle at Dorothy's desk.

Dorothy's gaze focused on the tulips Frank had already tossed in the trash. "You haven't heard?"

The paper ball missed the receptacle. "Haven't heard what?"

Dorothy's gaze shifted toward the newspaper article on her desk and reached for the tissue box she'd placed on her desk this morning as another prop. She withdrew a tissue and dabbed at her dry eyes. "Genevieve and Hunter are missing." She reached for another tissue and glanced in Lady Roselyn's direction. "Will you please tell Frank what you told me? I don't think I can."

"Did something happen to Genevieve?" Frank said.

Lady Roselyn fingered her brooch again, keeping to the script Genevieve and Hunter had sent them. "We're not one hundred percent positive. The tour arrived on schedule at the town, Civita, and soon after that there was an earthquake, stranding everyone in the city. A transport helicopter had to fly in to extract them. Everyone except Genevieve, Hunter, and my dear sister, Bridget. No one knows why they didn't make the transport, and now they are presumed missing."

Dorothy sniffled and blew her nose. "It doesn't feel real. Everything in Genevieve's life seemed to be coming together. You and she were engaged, my daughter was happy and had told me she was interested in taking on a more active role in running the newspaper. I don't know what I'm going to do."

Frank walked over and handed Dorothy the tissue box. "You have me. You don't have to worry about anything. If Genevieve and I had married, it would have been simpler. There is a solution, however. You know how much I love the newspaper. You could sign it over to me, and I'll make sure it runs like a top while everything is sorted out. You and David have too much to worry about right now. After an explosion like the one that destroyed Civita, it might be a while before they find any…survivors. Meanwhile, you and David could travel to Italy in case you're needed."

"Explosion?" Dorothy said, her eyes like twin

shards of glass. "I never mentioned that there was an explosion."

"I must have heard it on the news," Frank said, his eyes narrowing.

Genevieve emerged from a side door of the office. "Hello, Frank."

Frank blanched visibly and stumbled toward a chair, sitting down hard.

"It wasn't on the news," Genevieve said, "because there wasn't an explosion." She pulled up a chair beside him. "The only way you could think there would have been one was if you'd talked to Claude. By the way, Claude is in custody, and explained your involvement."

Lady Roselyn knew Genevieve was bluffing. They didn't have hard evidence against Frank. Their only chance was a confession. She fingered her brooch again. "We're planning to have you reunited with your friend Claude."

"The authorities can't arrest me simply because I used the word 'explosion' instead of earthquake. I doubt I can be charged, let alone have the case go to trial."

"Perhaps," Lady Roselyn said, working on a hunch, "but you're involved with Matchmaker Affairs now." She paused. "I'm curious. Did Claude tell you anything about us and our methods?"

His eyes widened as his gaze shifted to the door. He looked afraid. "A little."

"Then you know we don't work in the conventional way. If I tell the Matchmaker Council you cooperated, it will go easier for you."

He squirmed in his chair. "You have to let me go."

"And you know that I won't."

"Frank," Genevieve said, breaking into the conversation. "Why did you collaborate with Claude?"

He snapped around to Genevieve, his mouth pinched into an angry line. "It was your fault. Things were going according to plan, and then you had to change your mind and want to run the *Daily Beat* yourself."

"But we were going to run it together."

He rolled his eyes. "And likely make it a success. That would have destroyed my plans. I love that you never knew the truth, that you never made the connection. But then, how could you? You were a toddler when it happened. Your mother knew, of course, and I persuaded her to keep my secret. She was so proud I'd made something of myself after her newspaper destroyed my father's reputation and career when she exposed him for taking bribes to cover his gambling debts. I wanted to ruin your newspaper and drive it into bankruptcy, in the same way it had bankrupted my father."

Lady Roselyn shook her head. "But how was Claude involved?"

"I owed him a gambling debt. It seems that vice runs in the family. Claude promised to clear my debt if I persuaded you to join Hunter on the Matchmaker tour to Italy and prove that the sisters were thieves." He leaned back in his chair and closed his eyes. "I've told you what you wanted. What's next?"

Lady Roselyn stood. "I will keep my promise. The Matchmaker Council will know that you cooperated. It's time to go."

Chapter Forty-One

William had asked his driver to take him straight from the airport to the Matchmaker Café. They'd arrived over fifteen minutes ago. William was in no hurry. He'd rehearsed what he would say to Lady Roselyn regarding Claude. Would she see through his explanation? He was hoping her involvement with the upcoming wedding of Daisy and Jorvy would act as a distraction and she wouldn't ask too many questions. The more questions she asked, the more likelihood of her suspecting he was keeping secrets from her.

He glanced out the limo window by the passenger seat. The weather was unseasonably warm for Seattle; from the frying pan into the fire, as the saying went.

The return trip from Italy to the United States had been uneventful. He hadn't slept, but that was to be expected under the circumstances. He'd changed his tweed jacket on the plane. It was his favorite but beyond repair, sacrificed for a good cause when he'd escorted Claude to Scotland. After Claude's claim that Lady Roselyn and her sisters had been stealing artifacts for decades, maybe longer, Claude had arrived at the conclusion that William would help him escape.

On the sidewalk in front of the parked limo, a couple with a baby carriage strolled by. Quiet stuff. Normal stuff. Stuff that he'd never experienced.

He leaned against the seat and shut his eyes. He

had let Claude believe he'd work out the details in exchange for his silence. As soon as Claude had turned over information on the location of the stolen artifacts that had caused the doors to malfunction, William had granted Claude's wish to become as rich as a Midas. Claude was partial to the eighteenth century, and since he liked the idea of owning a castle in Scotland and having a title, William drew up the documents for Claude to sign, making him the laird of Castle Inverness.

William straightened his tie, got out of the limo, and dismissed his driver, hoping he'd done the right thing. He headed toward the café, past the couple with the baby, smiling a silent hello, and remembered how easy it had all been. Too easy, some would argue. He'd been careful. But sometimes, even with the best-laid plans, mistakes were inevitable.

When the men assigned to escort Claude to the Matchmaker Council had arrived at the villa in Italy, he'd explained that he'd been ordered to take Claude in himself. They hadn't objected. After all, William outranked them.

Would the council believe William's story? He'd promised to escort Claude through a door that led to the council's chamber, where Claude would be taken into custody for trial.

William would claim the door had malfunctioned. A plausible explanation.

And Claude hadn't made any objections, either. He believed William was helping him escape so that he could live out his life in luxury at a castle in Scotland where he'd reign as its laird. Instead, William had tricked Claude into opening the door to Culloden on

April sixteenth, in the year seventeen hundred and forty-six, the day the Scots were slaughtered by the English. Culloden had been one of the bloodiest battles in Scottish history. William had escorted the new Laird of Castle Inverness back in time and had made sure he was on Culloden's field when the battle began. William had barely made it back alive. Laird Claude had not.

He buried the battlefield screams in the hole in his soul where his nightmares dwelled. It was not the first time he'd been at Culloden.

William's hand trembled as he opened the café's door and headed toward the office, where he knew he'd find Lady Roselyn this time of the morning. He rationalized that what he'd done had been necessary. He didn't believe Claude's story that the sisters had been stealing from the past, but Claude could stir doubt, and if the Timekeepers grew nervous, they might shut down the matchmakers. Even now William wasn't sure if Duncan would launch his own investigation once he discovered Claude had never made it to the council's chamber.

Decorations for Daisy and Jorvy's wedding were stacked in boxes in the center of the café, waiting to be unpacked for tonight's celebration. He'd help as soon as he met with Lady Roselyn.

A pang of regret caught him off guard. He shook it aside as he entered her office. Remember your vow as Keeper of the Doors, he told himself. The enchanted doors must remain open. Nothing else mattered.

Lady Roselyn was alone, going over receipts. She glanced up when he approached. Her smile faded as though a cloud had passed over the sun. Did she suspect?

"What's wrong?" she said. "Did you have any trouble turning Claude over to the disciplinary council?"

William shook his head and pulled out a chair beside her.

She sighed in relief. "I worried, as Claude could charm the devil himself into believing his innocence, if given enough time. I once believed his lies and promises. I pray he's given the justice he deserves."

William fingered the fly pendant in his pocket that he'd taken from Claude. It lay beside the one Lady Roselyn had given him on the day he still believed in dreams. William reached for Lady Roselyn's hand and kissed the back of her fingers. "I promise. No one escapes Lady Justice."

Chapter Forty-Two

The Matchmaker Café was dressed for a party, celebrating the wedding of Daisy and Jorvy. Banners hung from the ceiling, full of congratulations to the bride and groom and reflecting the colors of summer. Chairs were draped in cheery sunflower yellow and meadow green, and vases of white and blush-pink hydrangeas were on all the tables.

And yet Genevieve couldn't shake her unease, although things in the Village seemed back to normal. Lady Roselyn had taken Frank into custody and promised that he wouldn't be harmed but he would learn his lesson, whatever that meant. She'd never seen her mother happier at work, and Genevieve's stepdad had offered to help Dorothy with the newspaper.

But after today she'd never see Hunter again. It shouldn't matter, she reasoned. True, they'd shared an enchanting moment together and had been caught up in the heady combination of the romance of Italy and the adrenaline rush of danger. They'd let their guard down. Now what?

They were back down to earth and back to normal. She'd go her way and he'd go his.

She swept her hair behind her bare shoulders. She'd worn her hair down and chosen a strapless red sheath for this occasion.

Hands shaking, she ducked back into the changing

room of the café. Lady Roselyn had planned the wedding as well as insisting the affair be formal. For those who said they had nothing to wear, she opened a walk-in closet the size of a palace ballroom, filled floor to ceiling with designer shoes and evening wear that would make a fashion magazine's staff drool.

The door was ajar. "Hunter, it's almost time for the guests to arrive. Are you ready?" She heard him talking on his cell and edged the door wider.

He ended the call, tucking his cell into the pants pocket of his tuxedo. He scooped up studs from the table and swore. "This is insane. Why would anyone want to wear clothes that are difficult to fasten? My shirt is starched as stiff as a board, and I swear the buttonholes are sewn shut." He dropped his hands to his sides. "Go on without me."

Genevieve crossed over toward him. "Oh, no, you don't." She took the jet-black studs from his hand. "I'll button your shirt. Daisy and Jorvy are our friends. We promised we'd be there, and that means you wearing a tux."

"I'd rather go naked." His eyebrow lifted as his eyes sparked with mischief. "Why don't we both go naked? As much as I like the dress you're wearing, I'd like it better if you took it off."

Why was he teasing her as though they were a couple? It was confusing. Her hand shook as she pulled his shirt together where it had been exposing a chiseled mass of abs. Her fingers grazed his warm skin, sending a jolt through her. She swallowed. "Neither one of us is getting naked."

He lifted his chin as she fastened the top stud in place. "The night is young," he said.

She concentrated on the next button. They were joking around as though they were a couple, as though they would see each other after the wedding. But they weren't a couple any longer. Their assignment was over, and he was leaving.

"You're making this more difficult than it has to be. Lots of men wear a tux."

"I agreed to wear this costume, but I don't have to like it."

"It's not a costume. It's formal wear."

"I know what it is. I had to wear something like this every Sunday when I visited my Gran for dinner."

Genevieve drew back. "Hold on. You had formal dinners when you were growing up? I thought you lived on the Makah Indian Reservation."

"Six days on the reservation and one day with Gran. That was the arrangement until I turned eighteen."

"So how is it you can't fasten your own shirt?" She paused. "No, that's not the first question I want answered. The only people I've heard about who dress formally for dinner are the insanely rich."

Hunter reached for the bowtie on the table. "Define insanely rich."

Genevieve clenched her hands at her sides. "How big was your house? Correction. Houses? Did you have private tutors, servants, gold toilets?" She crossed her arms over her chest. "And only someone rich asks the definition of 'insanely rich.' "

He stepped back from the mirror. "I'm ready."

"You tied your bowtie. It looks perfect. How did you do that?"

"I told you. Gran required that I dress formally for

dinner and special events."

"You went to special events? Did your Gran entertain politicians and ambassadors, or just kings of small nations?" She drummed her fingers on the arms she'd crossed over her chest. "You can tie a bowtie, which I've heard is not easy, yet you can't fasten your shirt. Explain."

He grinned. "That's easy. I wanted you close to me. You look gorgeous, by the way. I like your hair down. On another topic, I know you're looking forward to the wedding and staying for the reception, but we can't stay that long. When I was offered a new assignment, I checked with your mom. She said that the whole clandestine-style incident with Frank rejuvenated her, and she especially liked the idea of you doing more investigation with me. We leave tonight."

His words spun in her head, making her dizzy. "You talked to my mother? About an assignment?" She grabbed a chair to ground her. She was thrilled and confused and annoyed, all at the same time. She put her hands on her hips. "You should have asked me first, not my mother. Maybe I don't want to go with you. Did you think of that?"

"That's ridiculous. Of course you want to go with me. You are right, though. I've never had a partner, and as a result I did it out of sequence. I should have asked you first. When you came in, I was on the phone finalizing the arrangements for us with the guy in charge of a new investigation. He'd heard about what we did in Italy."

"Us? You mean…"

He cupped her face in his hands and kissed her on the mouth. The kiss was as light as mist, then deepened.

"Yes, us."

He said against her mouth, "You're stuck with me for one more assignment. Actually two. We have a stopover in Saudi Arabia first. Any objections?"

She smiled against his lips. "I'm sharing the byline."

He laughed. "I wouldn't have it any other way." He reached for her hand. "We'll make an entrance, congratulate the bride and groom after the ceremony, and then make our exit. The prince said he's ordered a limo that will take us to his private jet."

Genevieve pulled away. "A prince's private jet? I'm intrigued. Is he an English prince, African, or Middle Eastern?"

"I'll fill you in on the plane ride."

"You're friends with a prince?" Genevieve said. "Who are you? Really?"

"Titles aren't important."

"You have a title?"

A word about the author…

Pam Binder is an award-winning Amazon and *New York Times* bestselling author. Pam believes in smiles, Irish and Scottish myths, and like Wonder Woman, the power of love.

Pam writes historical fiction, contemporary fiction, middle grade, and fantasy.

Visit her at:

Website: www.pambinder.com
Twitter: PamBinder183
Facebook: pam.binder.5
Pinterest: pbinder183